THE KISS OF DEATH

Marcus Sedgwick

GALAXY

PLUS

First published in Great Britain in 2008 by
Orion, a division of the Orion Publishing
Group Ltd
This Large Print edition
published by
BBC Audiobooks 2009
by arrangement with
the Orion Publishing Group Ltd

ISBN 978 1405 663533

British Library Cataloguing in Publication Data available

Printed and bound in Great Britain by
CPI Antony Rowe, Chippenham and Eastbourne

THE KISS OF DEATH

For Ellie and Bob

THE LETTER

I have only one wish now, one . . . desire.

I want to be near you. I want, and I need, to reach out to you across this dark water that divides us and touch you. I want to be close to you, once again. Surely you can let me get close to you one last time? You owe me that, and you can't be afraid of me, so why not let me come and see you?

And then, when I have you in my arms, I know you will lean in towards me, so your lips will brush mine, but I will hold you a little tighter, and then I will put my hands up to your neck, and I will begin to squeeze. I will hold you until your feet have stopped shuffling on the wet paving stones, and your hands have stopped scrabbling against my arms and my face, and I will go on squeezing until your lips have stopped twitching and you are no more.

I will drop you into the water, where, for all you have done, you can rot.

Then, and only then, my friend, will I let you go. Then we will be done with each other, you and I.

Then we will be done.

I'm coming for you,
A.

ONE

1

Death can come in many forms, but in Venice, death comes by water.

*   *   *

The boy held the letter lightly between his fingers, and read the words written there, as he had read them twenty times a day for twenty days.

Marko stared at the handwriting. It was his father's elegant script, and he knew it was genuine. He could almost smell his father's scent on the paper. Smell the medicines from his surgery. Smell his mother's fear as he'd left the house, six months before.

*   *   *

Grimly Marko folded the letter back into nine and slipped it inside his coat. His eyes lifted to the dark horizon, and only now did his senses return to the heave of the boat, the swaying of the cordage around him.

Water slapped at the windward side of the caravel as it turned the headland and made for the islands. It was January, the air was icy and seething with damp. He was cold. Cold and tired, but he had not even begun to think about these things yet.

One page of a letter, and a strange one at that. It was not addressed to anyone, did not begin with any formal introductions, and yet it ended as a letter should. Everything not quite as it should be, and then there were the words themselves; words etched in thick rich splattering ink; words that spoke of hatred and bile, and the threat to kill. Marko did not recognise his father in among that violence, it spoke of a man so very different from the gentle doctor everyone knew him to be. But he knew the writing so well, as it was the writing he read everyday as he assisted in his father's surgery, mixing powders and dispensing potions for the sick of Piran.

*   *   *

The letter had arrived one day, almost three weeks ago, at their house in the hills. Marko had been wrestling with his eight younger brothers and sisters, trying to get at least one of them to wash, when his mother had come in clutching the letter. She'd broken the seal and was holding it out to Marko, a mixture of fear and curiosity on her face. It made no sense. Someone else, in a different hand, had written their address on the back of the paper, folded and sealed it to make it its own envelope, and sent it on its way.

There was another thing. A scrap of paper fell to the floor. Marko picked it up and read a few words, written hastily in the same hand as the address:

> *The doctor, Alessandro, has gone missing.*
> *We fear he may be dead. Come quickly.*
> *I will wait at the Leon Bianco.*
> *S. Bellini*

That was all.

Now Marko's heart began to sound the time of his arrival, and it was a late one.

'Hour till landfall!' called the ship's captain from the low deck behind where Marko clutched the rail.

'So long?' he asked a sailor who stood pulling on a rope near at hand.

The deckhand didn't bother to look round.

Marko tried again.

'So long as an hour? It looks so close.'

'But it's not,' spat the sailor in reply, too busy with his work to pay Marko much attention.

Marko looked out across the rail towards the horizon again. Dusk had fallen and all that remained of daylight was a faint green glow over the mountains way beyond the lagoon. He struggled to even make out the vague shape of the island city in the gloom. He didn't know much about the place, even though it was where his father had been born, where he'd grown up, trained as a physician, and practised medical arts for many years. Marko suddenly felt a stab of regret. Why had he never known more about his father? Should he have asked more questions, listened more? Perhaps, but perhaps the fault did not lie with him, but with his father.

So Marko only knew what his father had told him before he left, and the little he'd managed to glean from the letters he'd sent. Then the letters had stopped, for months on end, until the one arrived that had brought Marko here now, across the water in the gathering night, to Venice.

Words are not enough. Marko could clearly remember his father telling him about this strange city, and, as usual, his father had been right.

Marko had often travelled with his father, especially as the years had started to slow him down. Once a month they made the journey on horseback, over the hills from their little port of Piran, to the great massing sprawl that was Trieste. There, Marko would idle away a few hours in the square while his father concluded his business. Then, their saddle-bags full of herbs, spices, stones and dried animal parts, Marko would tear his eyes away from the long-legged girl who worked in the tavern and they'd set off home, arriving well into the dark hours of the morning. Marko, therefore, thought he knew what a city was like, and that all cities in the world must be more or less the same, but when the boat slipped like a wet ghost into the Venetian lagoon, he knew how wrong he'd been.

'Yes Father,' he muttered to himself, as the caravel drifted silently alongside the first buildings. 'Words are not enough.'

Someone slapped him on the back, and he turned to see Captain grinning at him.

'Think you're dreaming?'

Marko shook his head.

'I don't know. How does it . . . ? Why doesn't it . . . ? Who thought . . . ?'

Captain laughed.

'Of course, it's not the place it once was,' he said, mock serious. He was a decent man, Marko had decided. A spice trader, come to buy and sell in the city at the centre of the world, as he called it. He had a handsome face, but one that had fought the sun and salt for too long, and lost. Their journey had been three days from Trieste, and Marko had grown to like him, and like all the ship's hands, called him Captain. He'd been at sea so long he had no other name.

'Once they ruled the world, these people,' Captain said. 'Well, the seas, at least. If you wanted to trade anywhere from Barbary to Turkey you had to ask here first. Those days are gone, happily for me, but it's still enough to make most men weep.'

He sighed.

'What do you mean?' Marko asked.

'It's too much, this place. Too strong. It does for most people in the end. I wouldn't live here for all the salt in the sea. It's too beautiful, the wine's too potent, the stories are too frightening. The women are too friendly, the men too vicious. This city will suck you in and spit you back, inside out. I'm telling you this because you were a good passenger and earned our respect.'

'Telling me what?' Marko asked. The small ship drew closer to the walls of houses that seemed to stand right in the green-black water, thrusting up from the mud with elegance and indifference. In the half-light, Marko could see the outline of the rooftops, towers and domes of the skyline. Torches flickered in windows and archways, and their redness danced across the dark mirror of the water towards him.

'What are you telling me?' he repeated.

'Just to be careful. That's all. Be careful.'

7

Marko smiled.

'I will. I can look after myself.'

'Sure of it? I hope. You're strong enough, for your age. But some things aren't about strength, are they? I don't know what you're doing here, but if I were you I wouldn't stay too long.'

'How long is too long?' Marko asked, grinning.

Captain laughed.

'That's for you to find out,' he said, as he left, heading aft to mind the steering into harbour.

Marko had said nothing about the reason for his journey. He had money to buy his way across the sea, and that was all anyone cared about. No one on the ship had asked him what he was doing.

It had been one evening, after days of indecision, that he'd finally convinced his mother to let him go and find his father. It hadn't been easy.

'What if you never come back too, Marko?'

She must have said it a thousand times in those days before he left. And he knew she was right. Supposing he never did come back, and left her with the eight little ones to look after? Tomas, the oldest boy, was only eight, and Irina and Elena, the twins were twelve. The others were just babes really, and none of them earning a living.

But in the end, Marko had won.

'You'd have us give him up? Never even try to find him?'

Five days ago, he'd got up earlier than normal, dressed in his best clothes and stoutest boots, and then joined his mother at the big table in the kitchen. They counted out all the money they had left from his father's safe keeping.

'We'll halve it,' his mother had said, making two

8

piles. 'You'll need more than we will here. It's expensive to travel and to eat.'

'No, mother,' he said. 'There are nine of you and one of me. And the children need feeding.'

So they counted half of one half back into the pile of money that was to stay in the house in the hills above the port of Piran, and Marko had put the rest in a bag round his neck.

'You bring him back, Marko,' his mother said. 'Bring him back so I can wring his silly old neck.'

She tried to smile.

He kissed her, and she began to cry, then he waved at his brothers and sisters, who were fighting among themselves, and barely noticed him go.

3

Marko sat at a table in a gallery that ran round the high walls of the large open ground floor of the place he now knew to be the Leon Bianco. Below he watched the comings and goings of the hotel, and for the first time on his journey, he felt alone. Not only that, but a single seed of doubt germinated in his mind. What on earth was he doing here? There was no chance that he could find his father in this teeming, writhing city. He didn't even know his father's friend, the one he'd come to Venice to help. The letter had been from him, S. Bellini, the glass-maker. It occurred to Marko that the man could walk right past him and he wouldn't know him. All he knew was that he was in the right place, the White Lion, the Leon

Bianco.

*   *   *

Captain had brought Marko as far as the hotel. He seemed to have taken pity on the boy.

While the deck hands had unloaded their cargo onto the quayside, Captain stood with Marko. He scratched his head.

'The Leon Bianco, eh?' He glanced around at his men, then back at Marko. 'Give me five minutes to sort this lot out.'

*   *   *

Half an hour later, well into the evening, Marko and Captain had jumped aboard a long narrow boat, shaped like a sliver of fingernail, but painted black. They joined three other passengers, who each pressed a coin into the boatman's rough hand, and set off and out of the harbour. Marko noticed that one of these passengers, a tall man in a black cape, wore a plain white mask. Some disfigurement to conceal, presumably. The pox, or maybe a duelling scar.

The Captain chatted away single-handedly, and Marko took little notice. He stared as the boatman leaped up onto the covered stern of the boat and facing forwards, began to push on an oar held in some kind of ornate rowlock at his feet. In this way, he deftly flicked the boat from its mooring and into open water.

Captain caught his eye.

'He's a gondolier,' he explained. 'This is called a gondola.'

Marko nodded.

'See how he only rows on one side? So why aren't we going round in circles?'

Marko shook his head, then stared at the boat a little harder.

'It's not even,' he said. 'It's shaped like . . .'

'Like a banana!' Captain chuckled. He stopped. 'You do know what a banana is, don't you?'

But Marko shook his head again.

'Well, it's a type of fruit. And it's yellow, and it's shaped like a gondola!'

Briefly, Captain was pleased enough to stop talking, but then he was off again, uttering more words than Marko had heard him speak on their entire journey across the sea, and Marko realised the veteran sailor was excited by his return to Venice.

A few more strokes and the gondolier was propelling them towards the mouth of a river that seemed to cut into the heart of the city itself. All around them were countless other boats; hundreds of the tiny gondolas, some slightly larger versions with two oarsmen, and large ships, as large as Captain's caravel, which glided through the water as if guided by a magical hand.

People were everywhere, in boats, standing in windows and doorways, but something bothered Marko.

'Where are the streets?'

'You're on the main one right now,' Captain said.

'This river is a road?'

'It's not a river. It's a canal, the Canale Grande.'

'It's artificial?'

'This whole city is artificial. They say it was built

on marshes, over a thousand years ago. They were just simple fisher folk who lived on the mainland, until the Mongols began to rampage and murder along the coast. The fishermen went out into marshes and built some little huts on legs, and they never came back. Look! They're still here!'

He pointed at the extraordinarily magnificent buildings that stretched out of the water, five and six storeys high, and away down the length of the Canal.

'They built these houses onto the highest clumps of mud, building up, up, up, and they diverted the course of the rivers that flowed into the lagoon so it wouldn't silt up. That made the water deeper. Now look at them. The fishermen. The richest fishermen on earth.'

Marko nodded.

'You were right,' he said. 'What you said on the boat. I am dreaming. It can't be real. But aren't there any streets at all?'

'Small ones mostly. What you're looking at is a series of tiny islands, joined by bridges. On each island, there are streets just like anywhere, but they're very small, because they used as much ground as they could for building the palazzi. The houses.'

Marko returned to his reverie, while Captain talked and talked.

'Of course, we don't usually stop at the Leon Bianco. Bit grand for us. We usually put up at a little albergo by the harbour. But it's been a good trip and I am the captain, so when you said you were headed for the Leon, I thought to myself, why not? You deserve it, I thought. Do the men good to be out of my clutches for a while, eh?'

12

He went on in this way, until the gondola put in right beside the front of the Leon Bianco, and they stepped onto a wooden landing stage, then straight into the chaos of the tavern.

Almost immediately, Marko was on his own. The captain met a woman who he seemed to know very well, as they disappeared somewhere upstairs within seconds. Marko heard him talking to the woman as they went.

'Why not, I said to myself. You deserve it.'

*   *   *

A girl whisked by with a tray of glasses and a large wine jug held high above her head. Nearly bumping into her, Marko stepped back and fell over someone's boot. He landed flat on his back and lay winded for a moment. He stared up into the face of the owner of the boot. A very tall, very old man, dressed in black, with a black cape, pure white hair, and a deeply lined face towered over him. As Marko's breath returned, the man stooped and with one hand took Marko's arm and pulled him to his feet. Somehow, before he knew it, the old man had with unlikely strength set him upright again.

He spoke quietly.

'Take care how you fall.'

It was a strange thing to say, and he spoke too with a strange accent to his Italian, an accent that reminded Marko of his mother's home tongue far away in the mountains to the east. Then he was gone, and Marko decided to stop drawing attention to himself. He found a table up above the noise, in the gallery, and clutched the wine

13

he'd bought from a serving girl, a girl who was actually a woman twice his age.

'You want to watch it,' she said, as he fished in the bag at his neck for a coin.

Marko glanced up at her, and saw she meant well. She smiled.

'You shouldn't flash all that around. Not if you want to keep it. Hide it.'

Marko groaned to himself, as he pushed the money into her hand. His first night in the city and he was behaving like a fool from the countryside. He knew better than that. This place couldn't be any worse than Trieste, he told himself.

* * *

He watched the life of the Leon Bianco hustle by. The whole ground floor opened into one large tavern, with plenty of drinking, tables for eating, but also tables for doing business. Even at this late hour, he saw money changing hands between all sorts of different people. Something else struck him. He'd assumed the masked man in the gondola was hiding some deformity, but now he saw that almost one of every three people in the hotel wore a mask of some kind. He could remember his father telling him about Venice suffering from the pestilence. Marko had asked him if that was why he'd left Venice, but he'd simply shaken his head and changed the subject. Could all these people bear the ravages of plague?

No, he saw now that many of them removed their masks to drink, eat, or just to chat, and held them by the ribbons which secured them to the face. He watched as people came and went – some taking masks off, some putting them on. Some never removing them at all.

The whole place reeked of seedy affairs, of bad business, of violence, sex and money, and Marko wondered, if this was supposed to be a stylish place to stay, what the Captain's place by the harbour was like.

People drifted to the first floor and to the rooms of the hotel above and behind the waterfront, and almost hypnotised by the flow, Marko suddenly realised that he was tired.

His eyes grew heavy, his head fell forward onto his crossed arms, and he began to doze.

*   *   *

He woke to the sounds of laughter and shouting. People were jeering and sniggering. Marko looked down over the balcony and saw a rowdy group pushing someone around. He could see the figure in the centre now. He was clearly drunk, reeling around the circle of people, swinging his fists wildly and ineffectually. He shouted incoherently, and then someone pulled the hood of his cape from his head. With a shock Marko recognised the old man he'd bumped into earlier. It was hard to reconcile his powerful calm with the drunken creature swaying on the tavern floor. The laughter rose and rose, and then as the old man landed a punch on someone, more by accident than skill, the laughter turned to ugly taunts.

Marko looked around the room. He felt sorry for the old man, but it was none of his affair, after all. He couldn't afford to get involved. Across the room, at the bar, he saw someone pointing straight

15

at him, leaning over and talking to a girl dressed in black.

He felt uneasy, slightly sick from his broken sleep. Standing up, he began to push past the other tables in the gallery. The ruckus below grew louder and he heard two young men discussing the entertainment.

'What did he say?'

'Same as before. His Italian is dreadful, but he keeps shouting about vampires. Vampires in Venice!'

They broke into fits of laughter and Marko doubled his pace for the exit. He was too late. The girl from the bar stood at the head of the stairs blocking his way.

'Who are you?' she said. She was young, but not *so* young, Marko saw immediately, and was finely dressed; a black cape over a black silk dress, with long sleeves. She wore a hood to cover her head, but underneath he saw her black hair was braided in elaborate patterns.

'No one,' he said. 'I'm just leaving.'

He pushed past her, not caring this time that he was being rude, and set off down the stairs, but she called after him.

'Do you know Alessandro Foscari?'

That stopped Marko dead. He turned and made his way slowly back up the stairs towards her.

The noise from the fight downstairs was reaching a climax, and there were shouts from the street now too.

'Do you know Alessandro Foscari?' the girl repeated. 'Answer me quickly. We don't want to be here when the police arrive. They'll arrest anyone they don't like the look of.'

16

From her stare, she clearly meant Marko.

'Yes,' said Marko, 'I know Alessandro. He's my father.'

4

The girl was thrown, confused. Angry. 'They sent *you*? I've been coming here every night for two weeks, for *you*?'

She said something, obviously some curse, but Marko didn't understand. Her Italian was odd, he thought.

She sighed, looked at the fight, and made up her mind.

'Come on,' she said. 'We'd better be going. No, not that way.'

The girl grabbed Marko's arm, and they hurried deeper into the palazzo, down a steep flight of stairs, through a low doorway, and out into a courtyard. A fine mist had risen from the lagoon, hanging like a ghost over their heads as they rushed diagonally across the yard and into an alleyway so narrow they had to turn sideways to enter it. The girl led, twisting this way and that, and then they were in a wider paved street, but only for a second, as she turned another corner and headed back towards the water. Marko could smell it coming, and then they were at a flimsy landing stage on a small waterway.

The girl jumped into a gondola, and pulled Marko in after her. They sat opposite each other, Marko facing forwards, with the gondolier behind him.

'Don't we have to pay him?' he asked, nodding his head at the oarsman.

'No,' the girl said. 'He's ours.'

They pushed out of the narrow water and Marko saw they were back in the Canale Grande, but a few houses further down from the Leon Bianco.

'That was a neat trick,' he said, looking back at the hotel.

'Look,' she said, and Marko saw the fight spilling out into the doorway of the palazzo. Someone fell into the water and then there were more screams and angry shouts.

'The police have arrived.'

Marko turned back to her.

'I'm Marko.'

The girl said nothing, so he tried again.

'Who are you? How do you know my father? How did you know where to find me?'

'I wrote to you, to your mother,' the girl said. 'Remember?'

'The note was signed, yes. S. Bellini. Simono Bellini, my father's friend.'

'The note was from me, I assure you. My name is Sorrel Bellini, his daughter.'

'Sorrel? That doesn't sound very Italian.'

'No, and it's not Venetian either. It's an English name. I was born in London when my father worked for the King of England. My mother was English.'

'Was?' Marko asked, but regretted it. The answer was obvious enough.

'She's dead. She died years ago, when I was small. Then we came back to Venice.'

'I'm sorry,' Marko said.

18

'Why?' Sorrel said bluntly. 'Everyone dies in the end, don't they?'

Marko could think of no answer to that and they fell silent, as the gondolier pushed them out across the Canal, heading for a slender gap in the buildings in the far bank.

Marko stole glances at Sorrel. There was something so peculiar about her, he could see that already. His first glance had told him she was ugly, but his first glance had been wrong. He now realised that she was indeed very prctty, but what hid this was two things; her manner, and her make-up. Thick black rings of kohl circled her eyes, eyes which were actually a delightful green. That, and the scowl on her face, lent her the air of misery which had fooled Marko at first.

Around them, the water lifted and fell, gently, sucking at the flat bottom of the gondola; a real beast, but in elemental form. Cries of night-time in the city reached across to them, torches cast eerie shifting shadows on every side, and as the boat reached the far bank, they were eaten up whole by the massive palazzi of brick and stone that dwarfed the tiny waterway.

Barely wide enough for the gondola to pass, their speed dropped to a crawl.

'Where are we going?' Marko asked.

'Home,' Sorrel said.

Something in her voice again stopped Marko from saying anything more. After a moment, she spoke again.

'Home. To the House that Kills.'

Marko leaned forwards.

'What did you say?' he whispered.

Sorrel leaned towards him, and spoke in an

exaggerated whisper.

'They say there is a curse on my home,' she said, her eyes dancing with sick joy. 'There is a curse, and so they call it the "House that Kills". And that's where we're going.'

'You're joking.'

'Do you think so? I'm only telling you what they say. I don't believe in the curse.'

She stopped, then added, 'At least, I didn't.'

5

Squeezing between the buildings reminded Marko somehow of the forests behind their home in Piran. There was the same sense of entrapment, of being surrounded, hemmed in on all sides, unable to see more than a few yards, though here the trees were made of stone and the forest floor was made of water. But at last the little gondola was spewed out of the maze and emerged in open water.

The mist was thicker here and Marko suddenly doubted his sense.

'Where are we going? I've come to find my father. Why are we leaving the city?'

'We're not,' Sorrel said.

'But we're heading back into the lagoon.'

'No, we're not. Just watch the mist.'

Sorrel said something hurriedly to the gondolier, who chuckled strangely, but Marko didn't understand what she said.

'What language were you speaking? Italian?'

'We speak our own language here. It's Italian, sort of, but we have our own way with most things.'

'What did you say?'

'To Francesco? I told him to hurry up so the little boy didn't get scared.'

Sorrel looked him right in the eye, holding his gaze, daring him to be angry. He looked away, and over her shoulder, cursing her bitterness, cursing his ignorance and indecision.

'Where's my father?' he blurted out. 'What do you know about him?'

Sorrel put her head on one side as she answered him.

'I don't know where he is. That's why I sent for help. And they sent you!'

She fell silent again, staring moodily at the water. Marko opened his mouth to answer her back, but thought better of it.

*   *   *

She'd been right. Looming out of the mist was another island, which might have been a mirror of the one they'd just left.

'This is where we live. Giudecca. It's the shark that swims alongside the whale that is the rest of the city. Our palazzo is on the far side. We'll be there in minutes.'

Again the boat dove into the buildings, cutting through the heart of the island, but Marko soon saw what she meant about Giudecca – it was thin, its ends were out of sight in the mist. Within moments they were on the far side and there, finally, lay the lagoon itself. Marko could smell the cold wet wind from across the marshes, and knew the sea proper lay beyond all that.

'Our house,' Sorrel said, pointing over her

shoulder without turning.

'Which one? The one with all those people? Where the boats are?'

Sorrel stared at him, then spun round. She jumped to her feet and began to shout.

'Hey! What are you doing? Hey!'

Marko craned to see past her as their boat drew up to the house. There were four people, two men and two women, and three row-boats with oarsmen waiting. Luggage and parcels were being carried from the house and now the last were being piled up in the larger of the boats.

'Hey!' Sorrel called. 'What are you doing?'

One of the older men called back to her.

'We're leaving, Signorina. I'm sorry.'

'What do you mean, you're sorry? You can't leave. You just can't!'

'We're very sorry, but we won't stay another night.'

Sorrel jumped from the boat onto the thin strip of pavement at the water's edge and ran to them, pleading.

'Carlo, no! Maria, please. You can't leave us! Carlo, stop, talk to me, talk to me.'

But no one would even look her in the eyes as they climbed aboard and began to row away.

'Wait! Please. Come back!'

They didn't, and as Marko came to stand by her, she lost her temper entirely.

'You swine! You dogs! You . . .'

She let out a stream of curses and insults in Venetian dialect, whose meaning was clear, even if the words themselves were unknown to him.

Francesco had tied the boat to an iron ring set in the paving of the quayside, and gently put a

22

hand on Sorrel's shoulder.

She looked up at him and waved her hands at the departing boats.

'How *could* they? How could they?'

The tall boatman said nothing, but gently guided Sorrel to the front door of the palazzo.

'Who were they? Why are they leaving?' Marko asked, as she stood watching the boats disappear into the mist. The creak of the oars in the rowlocks drifted back across the water, even after they were out of sight.

'Well,' said Sorrel, still breathing heavily from her anger, 'That was our cook, her husband, the maid and the cook's boy. And they left because they are terrible, terrible people!'

She flung the last words into the mist where they fell dead on the water.

'What's the use?' she said, more to herself than Marko. She closed her eyes, then turned to look at Marko again. 'Come on, it's getting late. Have you eaten?'

'No, no. I'm starving, but . . .'

'But what? What! You want to know what's going on, you want to know what you're doing here. You want to know what's happened to your father. Well, so do I, and I want to know why they sent you and no one more useful, but I'm hungry, so let's eat first and talk later, yes? Especially as we'll have to get the food for ourselves now that the cook has run away!'

They went inside. Marko stood a step behind Sorrel in the huge entrance hall to the Ca' Bellini.

'Our family have lived here for centuries,' Sorrel said. 'Apart from my father's time in London. But then we came back. To this.'

23

Like a ghost she waved her hand in the faltering light shed by a vast candelabra suspended in the middle of the hall. It hung from a chain that stretched high up to the ceiling at the level of the second floor. What it illuminated was, Marko thought, like a dying animal. Some noble beast, like a wonderful stallion, but now on its last legs. What he saw spoke to him of years of wealth and grandeur, of commerce and opulence, exotic riches and domestic luxury, but which had all fled the scene, as mourners flee a funeral. That wealth and splendour was a thing of the past, what was left was a spectre of its former self; faded, rent, and sunken.

'It's incredible,' Marko said, though he knew that Sorrel knew he lied.

He stared at discoloured paintings, tattered rugs and tapestries, chipped chairs, the rotting staircase to the first floor, the grimy window glass. Wax from the candles had dripped to the floor, forming a series of small mountains of bizarre shapes that grew out of the Turkish carpet covering most of the hall. Marko had trouble pulling his eyes away from their grotesque deformities.

'And your father?' he asked. 'Is he here? When can I meet him?'

Sorrel's voice was as thin as the wind outside in the lagoon.

'You can't,' she said. 'That would not be . . . a very good idea.'

6

Why did you come?'

'You wrote to me.'

'I wrote to your family, to your mother.'

'She couldn't come. She has the children to look after.'

'So she sent another child instead?' Sorrel said viciously.

'You're no older than I am,' Marko replied defensively. Sorrel ignored him.

They sat in the dining room on the first floor, a room that spanned the whole width of the house. They'd chosen a small table by a window at the front of the house overlooking the lagoon, rather than the views across the roofs of other houses on Giudecca onto the city itself. Far away in the distance fires burned on some remote speck of mud, some excuse for an island.

'The mist must have lifted. In that direction at least.'

He pointed at the distant firelight.

Sorrel nodded vaguely.

They had not had to prepare their food after all; almost before they'd left the entrance hall Francesco had brought plates of cheese and bread and they'd followed him upstairs to the dining room.

'So,' Sorrel said. 'You're our cook as well as our boatman now?'

Francesco had nodded, and smiled.

'Won't you join us?' she added, but he bowed solemnly, and left them.

'Thank you, Francesco,' Sorrel called after him, so earnestly that Marko realised she was thanking him for more than fetching food.

Marko had no idea how old Francesco was. Not young like Sorrel, not old like his father, or that man in the Leon Bianco. He was somewhere in the middle. He had brown skin, presumably his birth colour and not a tan, given the dank and sunless winter in the lagoon. His face was only lined at the corners of his eyes, wrinkling when he smiled, which he seemed to do often.

'He doesn't say much,' Marko said once he'd left them to eat.

'He doesn't say anything,' Sorrel replied in her most withering voice. 'He's mute.'

'Oh?'

'He can't talk. He was a sailor, he fought with the Venetian navy, but they were captured by the Turks one day. He escaped, but without his tongue.'

She said it all calmly, as a matter of simple fact.

'That's awful.'

'Yes, it's awful,' she agreed, but again there was no emotion in her voice. She might have been speaking about the day's weather. Marko was reminded of what she'd said in the gondola, about everyone dying in the end. She seemed so . . . what was it exactly? Disinterested?

'It all happened a long time ago,' Sorrel explained. 'He was little older than you. Or me.'

She forced a faltering smile, and Marko knew it was an apology of sorts.

'Doesn't it cause trouble? Having a servant who can't speak.'

'If anything, it makes life easier. He never gets

26

involved with the others, with their arguments. Got involved, I should say. It's just me and him, now.'

'And your father?'

'Yes, and my father.'

There was another silence, and Marko was again left to wonder what the mystery about Simono was.

'And what about me?'

Sorrel put down her knife.

'I told you. You're no use to me. I'm sorry, I don't mean to be rude, but there it is.'

Marko restrained himself, but it was hard. He was still tired and the food had not worked any magic on him yet.

'And why,' he said, 'am I no use?'

'I meant for them to send someone, someone to investigate. Men. And they sent you, when what I need is a policeman.'

'They wouldn't send police across the sea to look for a missing doctor!' Marko said. 'What were you thinking? There was no one else who could come but me. If you wanted police why don't you get help from the authorities here?'

Sorrel laughed, and picked up an apple.

'This is Venice. The last people you want to turn to for help here are the police. Far too dangerous a strategy. You don't understand, you're not from here. Things are different here. No, I needed help from someone who knew your father, from someone who I could trust.'

'And you don't think you can trust me? His own son?'

Sorrel stopped eating and looked hard at Marko.

'Your father was from Venice originally, wasn't

he?'

'Yes, he left when my mother was heavy with me. We came to live in her homeland, across the sea.'

'So, you're half Venetian. Well, that may count for something. I suppose I have that much. But what can you do? Are you strong? Are you clever? Are you brave?'

Marko waited a moment before answering. He looked at the strange girl in front of him, with her woven hair and dark circles around her moody eyes. Her quick lips and sharp tongue.

'Sorrel, I don't know if I'm any of those things, but I'm something more useful than any of those. I'm angry, Sorrel. I'm angry. My father has gone missing. Without him my family, my mother, my three brothers and five sisters, will become destitute. You say he has gone missing. You even told us he might be dead. Someone is responsible for this, and I intend to find out who. And I'm angry enough to do it.'

He nearly added, so don't take me for a fool, but he could see he'd made his point, for Sorrel had turned to the window, trying to hide a tear that had formed in the corner of her eye.

7

What little joy there is in the girl, Marko thought. What little joy in this whole miserable place.

After they'd eaten, Sorrel had gone to bed.

'I can't talk any more tonight,' she'd said to Marko's protests. 'Please, let me be. I'm too tired.'

He'd relented, and she'd shown him a choice of bedrooms. After he'd seen six, he'd stopped her.

'This will do fine,' he said. They were all more or less the same. Each felt as though it had not been used in a hundred years, and there was little to distinguish between the mouldering state of one over another.

'Where's your room?' he added. 'In case I need anything?'

She looked curiously at him.

'But I thought you were brave, Marko,' she said, teasing. 'Very well. My room is that one, at the end of the corridor. And I'm going there now.'

She left him in his doorway and Marko watched as she shut her bedroom door behind her.

What little joy.

He undressed, then pulled the sheets from the bed and wrapped the coverlet around him like a cloak. His room was at the corner of the building, with windows to the front and side. He opened the shutters at the front for a few minutes. There, across the bay, he could still see that flickering firelight, and tried to work out which island it was coming from, then the cold got too much too bear, and he shut himself in again and lay on the bed, waiting for sleep to come.

It came swiftly and easily, like death comes in the night, and then he was gone far, far into the underworld of dreams.

Of nightmares.

8

The line between dream and nightmare is a fine one, and is easily crossed. Marko's mind replayed events in broken and disjointed segments. The arrival of the letter was mixed with his father's departure six months earlier, his journey on the caravel from Trieste became his gondola ride with Captain. He wondered where Captain was now, whether he was snoring soundly at the Leon Bianco, or had gone back to join his loving crew.

Sounds swished into range and out again. The lapping of the lagoon at the foot of the house. A footstep above his head, maybe, creeping in the corridor outside. The hoot of some night bird.

More visions muddled themselves in his drifting mind. Francesco became the old drunk from the tavern and they danced a minuet down the passageway outside his room, until the old man suddenly attacked Francesco brutally.

Marko saw a doorway, and it was Captain's doorway, and it was his own, right at the foot of his bed. He saw a crack in the old wooden panels, weakened by rot and worm, and through this crack a wild white eye glared into the room. It scanned this way and that, lids spun far back into the socket, as the eye flicked here and there, as if trying to soak the room up from beyond the door.

Somehow he knew in his dream that the owner of the eye was a woman, some ancient crone, withered with dry, pale, almost white skin, cold to the touch. He could tell all this from the eye alone. She was some sort of, yes, oh God! Some sort of witch. He moaned softly in his sleep, turned over, and drifted again.

*   *   *

Then there was screaming, and it was real screaming, which sank deep into the sleeping heart of Marko's brain, and was flung across the early morning waters of the lagoon, where it would hang for hours before finally evaporating.

Marko dived out of bed, winding a sheet around his waist. He staggered into the corridor. It was obvious where the screaming was coming from, it was a woman's screaming. There was only one voice in the house that high, and anyway, Sorrel's door stood open.

He rushed into the room, and found Sorrel with her back to him. In her hands she clutched a hand mirror.

'Sorrel! Sorrel! What's wrong?'

Sorrel turned and Marko's eyes widened with the shock.

Sorrel's face was an appalling sight. Her whole face was painted white, death white. The black circles she wore round her eyes had been worked outwards, enlarged into the hollow sockets of a skull, and her lips were hidden beneath a black patch the size of her fist that looked like the toothless gawp of a death mask.

She had stopped screaming now and began to wail uncontrollably.

'What have you done? Sorrel! What's the matter?'

She tried to hold back her cries, but still great heaving sobs dragged out of her mouth.

'Why did you do this?' Marko said, but all Sorrel did was point. At first he thought she was pointing at him, but then he realised she was pointing over his shoulder, behind him.

He was suddenly aware of someone standing behind him. Slowly, still moving as if in a nightmare, he turned, then leaped backwards, falling against the bed.

He swore.

There, no more than a hand's breadth away, was a man. An old man, his face painted with the same mocking death mask that Sorrel wore. His dreadful bloodshot eyes were wide open, and did not blink, nor did they focus, but stared straight across the room at the dull wall opposite. He wore a frightful white powdered wig, that might have been elegant once, but which now surrounded his head like the hair in a child's drawing, crazed and tangled. On his lips was fixed a rictus of a smile, thin and frozen.

In one hand he held a black stick of paint, in the other, a white one.

'Holy Mother!' Marko spluttered. His lips twitched with revulsion. 'Who the hell is that?'

Sorrel could only sob, and as Francesco's footsteps sounded in the corridor outside, Marko just had time to hear her choked reply.

'My father. It's my father.'

9

After Francesco had taken Simono back to his room, Sorrel began to calm down. Marko sat with

32

her, still wrapped in his sheet, until he began to shiver so badly that even Sorrel noticed.

'You can get into the bed,' she said, 'but stay down that end.'

She pointed to the foot of the bed and Marko gratefully climbed underneath the covers, pulling them around his shoulders as he did so.

'Are you all right, now?' he asked, but Sorrel didn't reply. She got out of bed properly, and lifting the hem of her long nightdress slightly so she didn't trip, she went to the washstand in the corner of the room, then returned carefully carrying a bowl of water and a bundle of flannel rags.

'Hold this, would you?' she said, and got back into bed. 'Thank you.'

Slowly, she began to dab and rub at the face paint. Her efforts only made it worse; the paint smeared into a worse vision than the death-mask her father had painted on her. Her face looked like a skull left out in the rain, that had somehow begun to dissolve.

'Let me do it,' Marko said, moving towards her.

'Stay where you are,' she said. 'Why aren't you dressed anyway?'

'I don't sleep in my clothes. It's cleaner not to. Especially when I've been wearing them for three days.'

She grunted.

'We'll get them washed.'

'Why did he do it?' Marko asked gently.

'What?'

'Why did your father do that to you?'

'He's done it before,' she said.

'That's not what I asked.'

Again she didn't answer his question directly, but at least she was talking.

'I was asleep, and dreaming that a spider was walking over my face. I brushed it off twice but it made no difference. Then I woke up and my father was leaning over me. He was looking right at me, but as if he couldn't see me. Does that make sense? Anyway, I knew what he'd done before so I grabbed a mirror. I don't know why it upset me so much.'

'Why does he do it?'

'To make me look like I'm dead.'

'But why would he do that?'

Now Sorrel became angry.

'Because he's mad, of course. My father is insane! Do you understand?'

Marko waited for Sorrel's anger to dissipate. She sat heaving in great sobbing breaths, but after a while she began to dab at her face again.

In the silence, Marko heard the sound of singing. A woman's voice, quite a decent voice, and though it missed a note here and there, there was an indescribable beauty about it.

'Who's that?' Marko asked. 'Someone here?'

'No, no. It's the lady who lives in the palazzo next door. Venetia. She arrived a couple of weeks ago to take part in the carnival.'

'What's the carnival?'

'You're so full of questions,' Sorrel said irritably.

'It's the best way to learn.'

'Maybe,' Sorrel said.

She picked up the mirror.

'Oh, I'm only making it worse.'

'It's greasepaint,' Marko said. 'You need cold cream, not water.'

Sorrel stopped what she was doing and looked at him.

'Yes, you're right, but how does a boy know that?'

She went to her dressing table and rummaged in a drawer, then returned with a small brown pot.

'I'm not only a doctor's son,' Marko said, 'but his assistant. I'm used to preparing creams and powders. You learn things, doing that.'

He stopped, something suddenly occurring to him.

'So, this is why my father came to Venice? To help your father?'

She nodded.

'He hasn't always been like this. This bad. Just the last few weeks. He knew he was getting ill, but he was still in his right mind. He wrote to your father and asked him to come, begged him to.'

'But they hadn't seen each other in almost twenty years, my father said. We couldn't understand why he'd leave us and cross the sea to help someone he didn't know any more.'

'There was a powerful connection between them. There is, I mean. That's all I know.'

'But why didn't you consult the doctors here? When your father got ill?'

'I told you. This is Venice. You no more want to consult a doctor here, than you would rely on the police. Oh, of course, they came, but my father dismissed them all, one by one. They were quacks and charlatans. They'd row up to the house, holding their hands out for their fee before they'd even come ashore. Then they'd swarm around him, diagnosing diseases no one's ever heard of, prescribing treatments that could possibly do more

35

harm than good. One told him to eat sheep dung every morning, and seaweed every night. Another told him to swim across the Canalazzo every day, then climb the campanile in San Marco.'

'What's the Canalazzo?'

'Sorry, the Canale Grande, that's what strangers call it.'

'And the campanile?'

'The bell tower in San Marco. San Marco is the heart of the city, the main square by the cathedral. Hah! I just realised. You are Marko, too. Is that why your father called you that? To remind him of the city he'd left?'

'I don't know,' Marko said, as if surprised. 'I've never been told.'

Sorrel smiled, then sighed and went on with her story.

'A third took one look at him and screamed that he had the plague. Then he ran back to his boat. It's not a good thing to say that word in this city. We've had too much of it. Anyone who knows anything knows my father doesn't have the plague.'

'So what *is* wrong with him? His physical symptoms, I mean.'

Sorrel looked at herself in the mirror, then looked at Marko.

'How do I look now?' she asked.

Beautiful, lovely, happy, sad, were the words that came to his mind, but what he said was, 'Fine.'

That seemed to be enough for her, and putting the things on the dresser, she came back to the bed. She stood, hesitating.

'What is it, Sorrel?' Marko asked. He sensed her unease. 'What is it?'

'I think the best way you can understand what's

36

going on, is this.'

She removed her pillow and then felt down behind and underneath the mattress by the head of the bed. For a moment she appeared to panic, then her hands found what they'd been searching for, and she pulled out a bound book, covered in soft hide, and tied shut with a taut leather cord.

She opened it, and leafed through the pages to about halfway, then held it out to Marko.

'I'm going to get dressed,' she said. 'And while I do, you take this back to your room and read. From this page. Then you'll understand. You want to know where your father is, and so do I, but you need to know this first.'

She passed the book to him.

'You can read, can't you?'

'Yes, of course I can,' Marko said. 'I am a doctor's assistant. I have to be able to read. Is it in Italian?'

'Venetian. But you'll get the idea. Take it away. I'll come for you when I'm dressed. Read, and then you'll understand.'

10

5th May 1682
The doctor has left and that is the last I will see of his kind. They are at a loss, I know that now, though I have not wanted to believe it so. The more they fail to understand what is happening to me, the more desperate and extreme their proclamations become. I will go forwards alone from here.

9th May 1682
After a few days respite from my condition, it
returned last night and gave me no peace
whatsoever. This morning I am pale, a haunted
reflection of my normal self.

12th May 1682
Still nothing will work for me. And I have tried
everything. My dear Aurora says I am trying too
hard, but I cannot stop myself. My heart pounds in
my chest and the blood beats in my brain, and the
more I crave them to stop, the harder their rhythm
becomes.
Four nights now.

13th May 1682
Five nights, and still nothing. Whatever I do fails.

15th May
My hair is growing thin, I think. Possibly. Certainly,
my eyes are pink and their veins shot through with
blood. My skin is feverish, my heart beats wildly,
and the pressure of blood in my body is giving me
fierce headaches. I look in the glass as I write, and I
see my pupils have shrunk to tiny pinpricks.
Yesterday I spent two hours reeling round the dining
room like a drunkard. Aurora thought me so, and
would not believe I had not drunk a single drop of
wine. And indeed I had not, though I love its taste so
much.

38

16th May 1682
*Eight nights now, eight days and nights, without a
single solitary moment.*
*I can bear it no more. I am ashamed to confess even
to these private pages that I have contemplated
ending my own torment, but I know I will not be able
to do it. Oh! How I wish I had that strength, and then
I could give myself what I crave, what is denied me.*

17th May 1682
*Sleep. Even the word, writing it, seeing it is torture to
me now. I cannot sleep. Ever. How is it possible? I
am dead, though I still stand on my feet. I am a
ghost, a spectre, a wraith. I am the mist that walks
on the water; I am the water itself. I am the foul
lagoon, and I am death's feather-wing that floats on
high and descends to sweep mortals into their
graves. I am death.*
But I am not sleep. Not sleep.

4th June 1682
*The miraculous change in the weather from that ill-
starred May to the beautiful sunshine of June has
marked a turning point for me, a wonderful thing! I
slept for four whole hours. That was four days ago. I
was so terrified it wouldn't happen again that I
didn't dare record it here, but last night, o joy! I slept
for nearly seven hours. Am I cured? Is it possible?
With the sunshine I see new hope. Aurora is so
beautiful in the sunshine, and this morning I was
able to show her how beautiful she is, for the first
time in months. She laughed as we kissed. And I
think, o God, that you have released me from my*

punishment. Praise be to God.

16th June 1682
How hateful I am! I cannot read the bitter words above without a knife stabbing my pounding heart. I spoke too rashly, indeed, and now I am four nights without a moment's rest. I have become a slave to this, an automaton, going through the actions of living as a real person does, but without the thinking and the feeling to make it real. At some moments Aurora tells me that I fall into a sort of stupor, with my eyes open and yet I appear to sense nothing, but these times give me no peace, no rest, and I know now that I will die for want of sleep. It is only a matter of when. My heart beats harder every day, the blood hurtles round my brain, but my soul is as grey and limp as the unseasonable mists that have returned to cling to the city day in, and day out.

17th June 1682
Though he is only seven years old, today I formally transferred ownership of the Ca' Bellini and the Bellini glass-shops to my only dear son, Simono. I have done all I can do for Aurora, and for my son, for the future, and I will be leaving soon.

19th June 1682
Yes. Swans. Or geese. Feathers anyway.

20th June 1682
How my cursed blood hurts me! Surges through the temple and the gut. My legs are iron, my eyes are hot

coals. The sweats are bad. Bad.

21st June 1682
Every thing has death. All is very clear to me this
evening. Every thing has death. The ancients
believed that only man had death. That a stone is
immortal, that a mountain, a river, the sun, are
immortal. Even the trees and the animals, the plants
and the birds are immortal. One bird may die, but
there is another! One plant may be eaten, but its seed
gives rise to another. Immortal. Only man has death,
the ancients thought, because only man knows that
he is going to die. That is the difference, I see that
now. Only man knows that he is going to die, and so
that must affect everything he does in life.
True? Or not?
　　That question, I cannot yet answer, but whether a
thing knows it or not, there is an end to every thing.
Even the stone, the flower, the river, the mountain.
All will be gone one day. Even this miserable misty
city will disappear one day, back to whence it came.
Back to the dark water.
　　Only man knows he is going to die, and I know my
death will be soon.

3rd July 1682
Sunshine. Glass. Aurora. Wine. Simono.

41

11

There, the diary ended.

Marko lifted his eyes from the book, his head still ringing with those mysterious last five words. The awful implication, left by half a diary of blank pages, was that death had come soon after. Marko hoped it was sooner, rather than later. Later would have meant more days of that torturous madness.

Holy God, Marko thought. What a way to die. Could there be anything worse in Death's arsenal than to die from lack of sleep? A total absence of rest that led inevitably to a massive failure of the heart, or a seizure of the brain. Sorrel said he would understand, but the book raised more questions than it answered. So, he knew his father had come to the city to try and help Simono, and he knew that Simono had the same disease that had killed his father, but it still didn't tell him anything about where his own father had gone. He had to get Sorrel to tell him more, if only she was more forthcoming. Whenever he asked her a direct question she would retreat into herself like a timid kitten hiding under a bed. He thought about his father, about the way he would deal with difficult patients.

'Get their confidence first,' he would say, 'Get them to like you. Then they'll tell you anything.'

That was what Marko had to do.

He got up, dimly aware of the singing from the neighbouring building again. He threw open all the shutters, then pulled the windows closed to keep out the cold. It was a foul morning, even hard to tell whether the sun had lifted itself into the sky, or not. A thick fog blanketed the whole city, a shroud of forgetting, Marko thought. Anything that had happened last night was gone today. Good, or evil.

The singing seemed close now, and a shutter opened in the building opposite. Only a small canal divided the two properties, and the window was on the same floor as Marko's room, so as he ducked back into the darkness of his room, he was able to see Venetia from very close range. She was so beautiful his heart nearly stopped its beating.

There was a knock at his door, and without waiting for an answer Sorrel came in.

'We found you these clothes. I think they'll fit, you can . . .'

She stopped, catching him spying from his window.

'Yes,' she said, an edge to her voice. 'She's beautiful. Everyone agrees.'

'No, I . . .' Marko said, feeling guilty, but vaguely wondering why that mattered.

'Yes, she's beautiful, but she's also a prize bitch. Just so you know.'

'Sorrel,' Marko said.

'What?'

He held up the diary.

'Your grandfather's?'

She nodded.

'Gentile Bellini. He was a great man.'

'He was a glass-maker, like your father?'

'He was the greatest glass-maker in Venice, which is to say he was the greatest glass-maker in the world. He died before my father was old enough to learn anything from him, and yet my father trained with one of Gentile's men, and went

43

on to achieve things that surpassed even those of my grandfather. His work took him across Europe, and eventually to London, where he worked for the King of England.'

'But he came back here. What happened?'

'The King had been a generous patron, but things change. Later, my father told me the King had got into some problems with investments in the South Seas. Many aristocrats were ruined. The King himself was immune of course, but could no longer be seen to spend vast sums on matters and objects deemed frivolous.'

'Your father's glass?'

'And so we came back here.'

'But I don't understand. The house. You believe this illness that befell your grandfather is the same one that is afflicting your father now?'

'Yes. And there have been other cases in the family. You read about Aurora?'

Marko nodded, but already had an awful premonition of what she was going to say.

'It took her not long afterwards. My father grew up an orphan. The richest orphan in the city. When he was old enough he took control of the glass factories on Murano. And there were others, even longer ago.'

'So if the house is doing this, why not move? Why do you stay here?'

'Believe me, we've tried. When we had to leave England, we lived in several places, but my father seemed broken by his experience with the King. He could get no work. We came back here, the family home. And there was something else. Despite what he said, my father seemed almost to want to come back here. As if he could go nowhere else.'

'Why not sell it and move somewhere else, somewhere smaller?'

'And tell me, who would buy the House that Kills? People shun this place, like a plague house. You saw for yourself last night. Even our servants have finally had enough.'

'But the curse . . .'

'So you believe in the curse already, do you? Hah! And you a doctor's son! And having got to know your father, you should be ashamed. Your father is a rational scientist, not some quack like the ones here. I give you this much, Marko, your father was the only man who seemed able to help my father at all. And that's why I want him back. We have to find him, find him before . . .'

Marko knew what she had been about to say, and the thought of her grandfather's end came back to him, but his pulse quickened at the mention of his father. He couldn't play this game of cat and mouse any longer.

'Where is he, Sorrel? When did you last see him?'

'About a month ago. They went somewhere. They wouldn't tell me where. That was the last time. My father was found the following day wandering round San Marco. They arrested him for drunkenness, and locked him up for the night. Then someone recognised him and brought him home.'

'And my father?'

'He never came back, at all,' Sorrel said bluntly. Then, almost as an afterthought, she added, 'I'm sorry.'

45

12

At the far end of a dead-end alleyway, a calle that led only to a short drop into a canal, a tall figure sat hunched under his black cape. He had pulled the hood over his face, and at a casual glance, even from a few paces away, looked like a bundle of cloth left out to rot. Maybe just a foot away you would see two eyes burning from under the black robes, eyes that seemed to sear the morning mist, through the stones and through Time itself, seeing happenings from long ago, and far, far away.

His eyes blinked shut as he thought about the night he'd passed, crouched in this stinking alley since the small hours, after endlessly wandering the city. He thought of the tavern and realised that even at his age he could still make stupid mistakes. He felt angry with himself. Surely he hadn't spent all these years travelling only to find he had learned nothing?

One mistake could still be his undoing, and he'd come too far and lost too much, to let it come to that. He thought about what he'd come for. What he was doing in this dreamlike place, and it gave him little satisfaction. Still, it had to be done. He'd spent his whole adult life for this, to find her. Find her and kill her.

*   *   *

His head twinged slightly from the drink, but he ignored it. To give it any welcome would to be to admit that he had drunk too much, though deep

46

down he knew he had. Why else would he have made such a fool of himself, and been thrown out, to spend the night like a beggar? He'd walked for hours through the deserted streets, crossing tiny canals by bridges without railings, getting himself thoroughly lost as if in a maze. He'd never known a place like it in all his years of travelling. Such a fantastical city, and that was something given the extraordinary places he'd been in his life, and the extraordinary things he'd seen.

He cursed. But it was the shame of losing his self control, not the damp cold that bothered him. He'd known cold all his life, and yes, this was a nasty wet coldness that sank into his bones, but it was nothing like the cold he'd known as a boy, the cold that he'd grown up with every winter, in the deep, deep forests.

He opened his eyes again, but he didn't see the dull red of the plaster wall across from where he sat. Instead, his vision was filled with a thousand memories, and every one of them was white, for they were memories of snow.

A Fairy Tale

There is a story as old as the moon and as dark as the night, a story from an ancient kingdom in the heart of a forest. It is just a story, but it is a terrible tale of love and death, and after all, what else is there? For these are the two pillars upon which life balances.

The King of this forest land was a good and just ruler, feared and respected, and it had been his blessing to have three daughters. In the course of the years, these little girls grew up to be fine young women, more beautiful than any other in the land; more elegant, more beautifully dressed, more refined. And yet, perhaps, more vain than any other girls in the kingdom, too.

Now the time came for the daughters to be married, and so the King held an enormous celebration, a festival that would last for thirty days and nights, during which time, all the suitable princes and noblemen from a thousand leagues around might come and ask for the hand of one or other of the princesses.

The festival began, with great pomp and great joy, as the King's subjects enjoyed day after day of feasting and dancing and happiness, and all at his expense. The suitors came from every kingdom, and a fine young bunch of men they were, and within ten days, the eldest daughter had found a man to match her, and consented to his proposal. They held the wedding that very night, and the festivities were

49

greater than ever.

Within another ten days, the middle daughter had also met her match, and that night another wonderful wedding feast was given.

But another ten days passed, and still the youngest daughter, who was perhaps the vainest of all three, was satisfied with no one. Many proud princes had ridden for days to come to the feast, and all but two had gone away empty-hearted. The King despaired, but on the last day of the celebrations, seven young princes arrived to seek the hand of the youngest, and some said most beautiful, of the three princesses.

One by one, the princes paraded before the princess, who sat on her throne, occasionally glancing away from her looking glass, to cast a bored eye over her suitors, and one by one, she turned them down.

The King was furious.

'I have thrown the most magnificent celebrations the world has ever seen. They have lasted for thirty days and thirty nights! You have seen as many potential husbands in that time, and each and every one a rich and handsome fellow, and still you are not satisfied!'

The King stormed about the hall, and everyone grew afraid, all but the princess herself, and then the King made a decision.

'Very well!' he roared. 'Since you cannot decide for yourself who is to be your husband, the fates will do it for you!'

He pointed to the back of the hall, to the great archway that led outside.

'Your husband will be the very next man to walk through that door!'

The hall was all astir, and every head and pair of

eyes within them, turned to peer towards the door.

Now, it just so happened that at that moment, a wandering tramp had been passing the castle, and hearing the festivities, had ambled in to see if he could beg for some food. Finding the castle grounds deserted, he made his way through the courtyard and towards the doors to the hall, and as he made his way inside, he was very surprised to see a hundred faces turning and facing him, as if they had all been waiting for him.

'There!' cried the King. 'Your husband!'

'Father!' the girl cried. 'No!'

TWO

Venice, the city that bears the name La Serennisima, 'the Most Serene', is a liar. For yes, she has a great beauty. From a distance, her reputation is great, her architecture is noble, and her people famed for the same quality. Get a little closer and much of this beauty remains intact, and unblemished. A rich couple stroll across San Marco, their expensive clothes gently whisking across the masegni, the paving stones of the city, their ornate masks sitting under even more ornate wigs. They are walking to a masked ball in a fabulous palazzo where they will dance and drink with other Venetian aristocrats. But come closer, look under the masks, take off the wigs. The woman is an old hag with thinning hair, too stupid to know she's not beautiful any more. Her face is gaudily painted. The ugly-intentioned man is her husband, but they ceased to be married in any real sense two decades ago. They prowl the night streets as foul and lecherous animals, throwing their money around casually in the hope it will attract some foolish and starry-eyed young beauty. Even the magnificent house they dance in is a fraud. It is a mere façade of elegance, and like the old couple, its face is cracked and lined. There is dirt and squalor in the dark corners of each room. The building is damp and rotting, and perilously weakened by it. It sits on a thousand soggy piles of Russian timber, all shoved down into the lagoon's black mud waters, where the waste from every water closet in the city now flows. It is a city floating in its own sewage, but it believes that it remains serene.

The Most Serene.

That is Venice.

2

The morning struggled to arrive, but finally a little light permeated the gloom of the lagoon mist. The city woke up. In the Doge's Palace all was chaos. The newly elected Doge was to make his triumphant procession in two day's time, and there was so much still to be done. Shipwrights tumbled out of their houses in the Arsenale to get back to work. There were the final repairs to make to the Bucintoro, the ceremonial barge, which would carry the Doge in full glory along the Canalazzo. On the island of Murano, away from the hubbub of the city itself, glass-makers were stoking their furnaces, coaxing white heat from glowing embers, happy that they would be warm today; probably the only citizens of Venice who would be. At the Leon Bianco, Captain staggered blinking into the sunlight, rubbing his head, cursing his stupidity at leaving his crew alone all night, and thinking of what he might have done the night before, apologised to his mother, even though she'd been dead for eight years. Upstairs in the inn, the ladies counted their money and brushed their hair, sighing over their lot, and pushed any sad thoughts away with fresh dreams of the luxury that might one day be theirs.

In the cluttered corner of a forgotten campo, yet

another body lay still, half hidden by rubbish. The only thing that moved was a slow pool of blood oozing from beneath it. Another random murder in Venice, though, had anyone known, this particular death was more sinister than a mere mugging, or some love-rivals' duel.

On Giudecca, a small boat tied up alongside the gondolas, and there was an argument over nothing between the gondoliers. In the house next door, across the tiny canal, Venetia stroked her long golden hair with an ivory and hog's bristle hairbrush, admiring her long neck in the looking glass by her bed.

And in the House that Kills, Marko sat with Sorrel in her room, as she talked about her father, and he realised suddenly that his life had changed. Whatever happened now, things would never be the same. His own father might be dead. He was miles from home, far across the water, with a girl he'd only met the night before, whose father, the sole link he had to his own father's disappearance, was a madman.

Things will happen that I won't want to happen, he thought. I will see things I don't want to see, and know things I don't want to know, before this is over. And what then? What will 'over' mean?

He shook himself. It's her, he told himself. Sorrel was affecting him. *Infecting* him, with her own special brand of misery. And this city with its clinging fogs, that was infecting him too. He shuddered.

'How long?' he asked her, interrupting her.
'What?'
'How long have you been like this?'
She stiffened.

'Like what?'

'So . . . black. So miserable, so full of . . .'

'Of what? Pain?'

'Yes, I suppose so . . .'

'Maybe since my mother died. When I watched her die. Or maybe when I had to come back and live in this rotting pile. Or maybe when I knew my father was going to die, slowly, right in front of my eyes. Which of those do you think it was? You decide. I don't care.'

She was full of anger and bile, and Marko regretted his words. He felt stupid, like an idiotic child, for having broken her reverie. At least she'd been talking. Now she was just fighting.

He got up, took a deep breath, and walked around her room, peering through grimy glass over the lagoon. His mind drifted out with the tide and back again, and his attention was caught by a bottle on the windowsill. It was small and blue, and some habit from his father made him pick it up and remove the stopper. He sniffed it, his nose wrinkled, then he saw Sorrel staring; he pushed the stopper back and returned the bottle to the windowsill.

Marko turned away and idly gazed at the bookshelf next to the window. His eyes skipped across the titles and he began to slide out the largest and oldest looking book, a leather bound tome without words on cover or spine.

'Put that back,' Sorrel said, but without anger.

'Why . . . ?'

He hesitated, the book half drawn from the shelf.

'Just put it back.'

Marko did as he was told, sliding it back into

position among the others, and Sorrel came and stood by him, seeming to want to explain herself.

'My father gave it to me, before he was . . . like this.'

'What is it?'

'The Pentameron. It's full of stories. They were written a hundred years ago by a man called Giambattista Basile. My father loves them. He gave me that book for my last birthday.'

She turned, moving back to the bed. Marko saw that she was trying not to cry. He walked over to her and sat by her on the bed. She was dressed in black again, another black dress, with a lower neck than the previous one, but with black lace cuffs to the long sleeves. Again, she'd woven her hair into extraordinary ropes of plaits, which she had pinned into wonderful patterns. Tentatively he put a hand on her shoulder. She sprang up from the bed, shaking her head.

'No!' she said. 'Don't do that. This isn't good enough. We have to start doing something, not just sit around here.'

'I thought I was no use to you,' Marko said.

Sorrel opened her mouth to say something, then stopped.

'Do you think my father is still alive?' Marko asked.

'I don't know. I hope so.'

'Because you think he can save your father?'

'He was so much better when Alessandro was here. He hadn't been out of the house for days. It had been awful, Marko. You have no idea. He would stagger around like a drunkard. He was sweating all the time, despite the cold weather. We brought him clean shirts five, six, seven times a day. They said it was the plague, they said it was a fever, but they were wrong. He'd fall into a kind of stupor, but with his eyes open, or he'd walk about with his eyes shut. Then, when Alessandro came, he started to get better. I'm sure of it. He even slept for half an hour one morning, and the change in him from just that was wonderful. Then one day Alessandro said he was going to take my father out, that they had to go somewhere. And then . . .'

'Your father went mad, and mine went missing.'

Sorrel nodded.

'Where did they go?'

'I don't know.'

'Didn't they say?'

'They wouldn't tell me, but I know it had something to do with business.'

'Glass-making?'

'Yes. We have the house, but we need money to live on. My father hadn't worked in weeks. He has a workshop on Murano, that's where all the glass is made. Your father said he had an order to complete, and that anyway it would be good for him to stir from the house for a while.'

'So they went to Murano? To see a customer?'

'Not necessarily. That's where my father makes his glass, but the customer could have been anywhere in the city. Or beyond the city.'

'But haven't you been to Murano? To ask about? Maybe someone saw them.'

Sorrel shook her head.

'I was waiting. I was waiting for help. I sent the letter so someone would come.'

Marko bit his tongue.

'Why,' he said as softly as he could, 'did you wait? Why didn't you go yourself?'

60

She lifted her gaze from the floor and held his eye briefly.

'Because I'm scared, Marko. I'm so scared.'

She looked away again and something in her manner sent a shiver up Marko's spine, making the hairs stand up on the back of his neck.

*   *   *

A little while later, they left the room, closing the door on Sorrel's small world of pain. On the shelf by the window, the books sat waiting for someone to open them, and in their midst lurked the Pentameron, and neither Marko nor Sorrel knew that sticking out of the pages, hidden from view against the wall, was a sheet of paper which had gone astray, and on which their destiny was written.

3

Marko and Sorrel stood on the fondamente, at the water's edge, outside the Ca' Bellini, waiting for a boat to the city to come by.

'Why don't you ask Francesco to take us?' Marko asked.

'Not in a gondola. Murano's too far. And anyway, someone must stay with Father. We can't leave him alone for that long.'

'Yes, of course,' Marko agreed. 'My God, it's so cold this morning.'

'It's the damp air. It chills your bones.'

Marko was about to say something in reply

when he became aware of someone sliding past him and squaring up to Sorrel.

'I want to see your father.'

It was Venetia. Marko stepped back a pace; she'd stepped between them as if he wasn't there, and he was thrown by her sudden presence.

'Your father took my money weeks ago. I shall have what I've paid for.'

Her voice was surprising; bitter and sharp and not what Marko expected to hear from such a lovely form.

'I'm sorry,' Sorrel was saying. 'I know he's been working on your tiara. He's spoken about it often. I'm sure it won't be long.'

'The procession is the day after tomorrow. I must have it for the procession.'

'Of course. I'm sorry. It's just taken a little longer. It's such a fine piece after all. It will be worth the wait.'

'It had better be,' Venetia snapped. 'Because if I don't have it by tomorrow night, and if I am not absolutely satisfied with it, then I will report your father to the Ten. Or the Three! And your father will be locked up as a fraud and a criminal.'

Venetia paused. Her lovely oval eyes narrowed to slits.

'Is your father—here?'

Sorrel hesitated.

'He's at his workshop.'

'Really? I haven't seen him leave the house for days. Are you sure he isn't here? I want to speak to him.'

'No!' said Sorrel.

'Why not?'

'Because he's not here,' Marko said, stepping in.

'You heard Sorrel. He's busy at his workshop.'

Venetia turned, as if only now aware of Marko. She looked him up and down, once, then again, very slowly. Her lip curled.

'And why,' she said, 'do you think this is any of your business?'

'This is my cousin, Marko,' Sorrel said. 'Father's on Murano, working on your tiara. We're going there now. We'll see how it's going. And there's a boat coming, we must hurry. I promise it will be ready for you. I promise.'

She dragged Marko along the quay and they almost threw themselves aboard the traghetto that would take them across the water.

Venetia spun on her heels and walked back to her house.

They watched her go as they bobbed across the water towards the city.

'I see what you mean,' Marko said, and Sorrel laughed despite her mood.

'What was she asking about, anyway?'

'She commissioned a tiara from Father, the very day she arrived in Venice. It's one of his specialties. He makes fantastic glass tiaras for ladies to wear at special occasions. They're so amazing, and so sought after, that they're worth as much as something made with diamonds or pearls. She paid him on the spot, there and then. And then his illness came back worse again.'

Her face fell.

'Now it will never be ready and she'll have him arrested. Even if we find your father, that tiara will never be ready for Venetia.'

'What's happening, what's so important?'

'It's the Doge,' she said. 'The new one. He's the

63

ruler of the city. Sort of. He doesn't actually do very much. There's the Great Council, and the Council of Ten. And the Three.'

'Who are the Three?'

'Shush!' Sorrel hissed, then whispered to him, glancing towards the other passengers.

'The Inquisitors. They have spies everywhere. They're best avoided.'

Marko nodded.

'So what about the Doge?'

'They've elected a new one. It's taken months. Anyway, he's declared there will be three days of festivities to mark his election, and a parade around San Marco. All the rich ladies will try to outdo each other, try and look the best, wear the best clothes. It's even more serious for the young, unmarried ones. That's why Venetia wants the tiara.'

'To attract a husband?'

'To attract a rich husband.'

'But she seems to be very rich anyway.'

'That's the thing about rich people. They always want to be richer.'

They fell silent for a while until the boat started to put in to the jetty at San Marco.

'Aren't we going to the island? Murano?'

'Yes,' Sorrel said. 'But it's away on the other side of the city, quite a long way into the lagoon. We'll walk across the city and take a bigger boat from there.'

They stepped up onto the stones of the piazzetta, the smaller of the two squares that approached the church of San Marco itself.

'This is where it will all happen,' Sorrel said. 'The procession of the Doge. That's his palace there. On the corner.'

She pointed, but Marko was already staring at the incredible building, intricate and ornate, dozens of slender columns holding up a façade of delicate brickwork, magnificent windows and little turrets.

The piazzetta was alive with activity; hundreds, if not thousands of people in throngs, shouting, laughing, trading, jeering, walking, staring and hurrying about their business. Nearby, a group stood around a low stage, from which two men addressed the crowd. They seemed to be both selling something, and acting out some kind of performance, but around them on a pair of trestle tables was a scene that Marko was very familiar with. Dozens of pots, jars, dishes and mixing instruments lay scattered on the tables. There was an elaborate set of scales, and one of the men was holding up a series of jars, extracting bids from the onlookers for their purchase.

'Teriaca!' the man cried. 'What will you give me for this wonder of the gods? It's the mystical medicine, the Venetian Panacea. Cures all ills! Protects against poisoning! Brings an easy sleep! Teriaca. There is nothing else on earth that can compete with its health-giving properties. You sir! Yes, you, you look like you could do with a little pepper in your pipe!'

The crowd laughed and cheered, and Sorrel pulled Marko away.

The teriaca merchant handed a green bottle with a cork and waxed stopper to a woman in the crowd, taking a jingle of coins into his hand from her. She hurried away, nursing the bottle as if it was a small injured animal.

Sorrel led the way past the palace, and Marko followed, his head spinning as he craned his neck to stare to the top of an enormous bell tower on his left. Some workmen were hanging about at its foot, and shouting up to the men near the summit of the tower. Various ropes and pulleys hung underneath where they clung to the tower.

As he passed, an elderly man clapped his hands in delight, and addressed Marko as if they were old friends.

'The Flight of the Turk!' he cried. 'Oh yes!'

He went gleefully on his way, and Marko saw him accost the next person with the very same exclamation.

'The Flight of the Turk!'

Sorrel was leaving him behind. He felt stupid again, an ignorant country boy, and he determined to stop acting like it. He hurried after her as she slipped out of the far corner of the piazza near a large and particularly hideous looking cathedral.

The square had been busy, with people coming and going, workmen going about their business, and street vendors shouting their wares, but now, a few steps away, the city seemed deserted.

In a few further steps, Marko realised he was utterly lost, or would have been without Sorrel. She flitted ahead, taking a turning here on the left, another to the right. It seemed impossible to walk in a straight line for more than ten yards, before the narrow streets ran into seeming dead ends, forcing them into alleys and over bridges, or sidling through some dark passageway that might suddenly open into a campo, a small square, a field of stones.

The sky was a grey blanket, glimpsed

occasionally beyond the high walls of the labyrinth that surrounded them.

'Are you sure you know where you're going?' Marko asked, but Sorrel clearly did, and she either hadn't heard, or simply didn't bother to reply. She seemed desperate to get through the city as fast as possible, and now their route took them over a small footbridge with no hand rails. The water beneath was foul and still. It made Marko think of some monster or snake, lurking, and he quickened his pace over the wooden arch, ignoring the danger of slipping on its smooth worn and wet surface. They entered a series of claustrophobic alleys, each of which ran for no more than a few yards, before turning at right angles into the next. The walls of the houses pressed in on them from either side, windowless and bare, and suddenly as Marko turned a corner, hurrying after Sorrel, she was gone.

He'd only been a few feet behind, but there were two options open to him, a turning ahead and to the left, and one to the right. He panicked, knowing he had to choose quickly, or even the correct choice might leave him stranded as Sorrel left him far behind.

'Sorrel?'

He called out. Nothing.

'Sorrel?'

Still nothing. For a moment he thought he heard footsteps, but if anything, they seemed to be coming from behind him. He held his breath and the sound disappeared.

Quickly, he stuck his head round the right hand opening, and saw nothing but a long passageway ahead, so he tried the left hand one. Again there was no one in sight, but he reasoned that Sorrel couldn't have got out of sight in the long right hand corridor so quickly. He took the turning to his left and began to run, as fast as the narrow bends would allow, and then, with relief he saw Sorrel waiting for him at the next corner.

He began to smile, but she cut him dead.

'I told you you're no use to me. You can't even keep up.'

'That's not fair. This place is crazy. And I'm used to having a sun in the sky to navigate by.'

She shrugged and set off again, turning more corners, and Marko was suddenly struck with the ridiculous notion that it was the city guiding them, rather than Sorrel knowing the way. He stirred himself as she entered a long alley, amazingly straight after the twisting maze they had just been through. It led away, and at the end Marko could see daylight, but once again the walls leaned in on them from above, so close that three storeys up they nearly brushed against each other. Ahead, the alley pinched to the width of a narrow waist, and then they squeezed through onto the wide pavement on the northern banks of the city.

Out in the lagoon, Marko saw a small island.

'Is that it?'

'No, that's San Cristoforo and San Michele. Two islands, one behind the other. Murano is twice as far.'

She pointed.

'Come here. Look. There.'

Marko followed her outstretched arm.

'Murano.'

Through the mist that hovered a few feet above the water, through the murk, it was just possible to make out the grey shape of another, larger island. But he might have been imagining it, it was so indistinct.

Marko thought he heard something behind them, and turned, but there was no one there, nothing but the mouth of the tiny alley from which they'd emerged.

A large lagoon boat was making ready to put out to Murano, and they hurried on board with the last of the passengers.

'Have you got money?' Marko asked, thinking that they'd already paid for one boat journey, mindful of his own dwindling supply of coins.

'I've brought all I could find in the house,' Sorrel whispered. 'It's enough.'

The boat heaved away from the fondamente, its nose drifting slowly round to point to the islands. As it went, a tall figure stepped from the end of the alleyway, and watched them go, then retreated into the darkness once more.

4

The boat appeared to make hardly any progress at all, and yet imperceptibly, Marko could tell that the city was moving further away. The smudge of Murano had disappeared altogether now, and they seemed to be heading for oblivion.

They sat opposite each other on low wooden boards that served as seats. The boat was almost empty.

Marko watched Sorrel for a long while. She gazed forward intently, as if her salvation lay there,

69

though there was nothing at all to see.

'You can't see forward,' Marko said. 'You can't see the future.'

She turned away from the future to look at him.

'What do you mean?'

'Nothing. Nothing much. About what I said before. In your bedroom. I'm sorry I upset you.'

Sorrel nodded, but didn't give him the satisfaction of accepting his apology.

'I'm sorry,' he went on, 'but you're so sad. You hide behind your black eyes, but I can see past the make-up.'

'What of it?' she asked cautiously.

'I can't explain this exactly,' he said. 'But suppose things don't end up as badly as you think they might? Maybe we can find my father, and he can make your father well again. Things wouldn't be so bad.'

She nodded again, but didn't seem prepared to speak.

'And then, if that happens, things will be all right. So what I mean is, why spend time now, thinking that the worst is going to happen, when it might not? It won't change what happens, but you're killing yourself simply with the fear of what might be. You can't change the world, but perhaps you can change how you feel about it.'

Marko stopped, wondering if Sorrel understood anything he was saying, whether she agreed with any of it. She looked out to the mist again, and then turned back to him. She spoke softly, but her words were full of crawling pain.

'The world is a vampire,' she said, 'sent to drain us of our souls. Our spirits, our joys, our happiness. And when it has finished, it leaves us gasping against the horror it has replaced those things with. We struggle, but we choke on that bile, and then we go spluttering to our grave. That is the world.'

She turned back to the sea again, and now, at last, Marko knew there was no point trying to reach out to her. He knew it was in his nature, since it was in his father's nature, to try and help people, to make them better. If they could not be made better, then at least their suffering could be eased while they waited for the end.

But with Sorrel there was no point, no hope. She didn't want to be helped.

'Very well,' Marko said aloud, but so quietly that she didn't hear.

There was no point helping this miserable girl, but he might be able to use her to find his father, and sail away from this rotting carcass of a city, back to their home in the hills, in the glorious, warming, forgiving, healing sunshine.

5

'So where do we go?'

'I don't know. It was your idea to come here. We don't know this is where they came.'

'We have no other path to follow,' Marko said. 'Where's your father's workshop? Is there someone there we can talk to?'

'It's at the far end of the fondamente. There's the foreman. Pietro. I don't like him.'

'Do you like anyone?' Marko said flippantly.

'Not especially,' Sorrel said, with a withering

look.

Marko rolled his eyes, and despite her venom, he smiled.

'Come on, then.'

It was hard to believe Murano had anything to do with Venice. Here, the buildings were all single storey, simple houses, very like the houses in Piran that Marko was familiar with. They were painted bright colours, reds, yellows and blues, so the fisherman who lived in them could see them from a distance through the frequent winter mists. Marko couldn't see that it would help much, but it certainly gave the town a more easy-going, informal atmosphere than the imposing nature of Venice.

As they passed various open doorways, Marko caught glimpses of roaring furnaces belching fire in the dark interiors of workshops.

'There,' Sorrel said, pointing to an archway that led away from the canal which bisected the island. They hurried down an alleyway and from the painted sign above the door, Marko knew they'd walked into the workshop of Simono Bellini.

'What do you want?' barked a voice.

They turned to see a squat, ugly man glaring at them. He stood by the open doors of the furnace, naked from the waist up, seemingly unaware of the enormous heat pouring from inside. His body was brown and greatly scarred, and though he was short, he had tough muscles on his chest and arms. In one hand he held a pair of forceps still glowing from having been in the jaws of the furnace.

'What do you want? Clear off!'

'Pietro,' Sorrel said, coming a little closer. 'It's me, Sorrel.'

The man squinted through the gloom and heat haze.

'Sorrel? Where's your father, then? Tell me that.'

He was either angry, or rude, or both. It was hard to tell.

'He's not well,' Marko said. 'But we've come to see you instead.'

'And who's this?' Pietro asked Sorrel, waving the forceps aggressively towards Marko.

'My cousin,' she said. It was as good a lie as any to keep using, and they both sensed that there was no reason to explain everything to everyone.

Pietro grunted.

'Where's your father? We want paying.'

'We told you. He's ill. I'm sorry you and the men haven't been paid in a while. I'll talk to Father when . . .'

'Well, there's only me left now, so don't worry about anyone else. All the others left. Men and boys. Gone to work for people who'll pay them. So just tell your father I want paying. And if not, then I'm going to go to the Council and have this place made mine. I've worked without pay for two months now. I'm owed something, and the only reason I'm still here is to see I get it.'

'Please,' Marko said, daring to step a little closer. 'I promise we'll get you your money, if you can just help us. We're trying to find someone.'

Pietro squinted some more.

'What of it?' he said.

'Can you tell us, when did you last see Simono? Did he come here, about a month ago? We think he might have come here, to see a customer, perhaps.'

73

Pietro shook his head.

'No,' he said. 'There was no customer. But he did come. With another man. He wasn't a customer. I'd not seen him before.'

Marko's hopes began to lift.

'Describe him. This other man.'

'Tall, old. Old like Simono. Strong face.'

'Did you hear his name?'

Pietro shook his head.

'No, no. Unless, it was something like . . . oh. It could have been Sandro.'

'Yes!' cried Marko, turning to Sorrel. 'That's him. Alessandro.'

'So they came here,' Sorrel said. 'Did they talk about what they were doing, where they were going to next?'

Pietro shook his head.

'They went into the office. In five minutes they were out again. Then they left.'

'So why did they come?'

'Not to pay me, I can tell you that,' Pietro spat.

'We'll get your money.'

'I want it now,' Pietro said, and took a step towards them. He still held the forceps in one hand, and his body was running with sweat from the incredible heat. In the furnace light he looked like a cross between a dwarf and a devil, and they backed away slowly until he cornered them.

'I want paying now, Signorina,' he said.

Sorrel swallowed hard, Marko didn't dare take his eyes off Pietro, off the iron tool in his hand.

'Very well,' she said.

Bravely, she turned her back on Pietro and fished around inside the neck of her dress. She counted out a few coins from a bag, and then,

74

putting the bag away, she held them out to her father's foreman of works.

'It's all I can manage,' she said, trying to sound confident.

'Is it?' he said. 'Is it?'

He took the money, and slid it quickly into his pocket.

'But you must tell us what you know,' Marko said. 'What they did here.'

Pietro glared at Marko, who expected the forceps to come swinging towards his head at any second. But Pietro stepped back, smiling.

'Yes. Fair enough. Since you've paid me some of what I'm owed. But you tell your father I want the rest soon, or I'll take this place for my own.'

'All right. All right. But please tell us.'

'I said. They came and they went. It was all very quick. But they left with a box. Not too big. I think it was something Simono had been working on for a while. You know what he's like. Often works in secret on his special pieces. We never see them.'

Marko looked at Sorrel, and could see the same thought had crossed her mind, too. Could it be Venetia's tiara? If so, then one small problem might be solved.

'But where did they take it?' Sorrel persisted.

Pietro paused.

'Maybe they took it . . .' he said uncertainly. 'That is, I think perhaps they took it to San Michele. I heard them talking, when they were in the office.'

He looked furtive, he had obviously been eavesdropping.

'And they went to San Michele?'

'I'm not sure. But I heard them mention the

church of San Michele. There's a priest who lives there. We've done work for him before.'

'For a priest?' Marko asked.

Sorrel ignored him.

'You think that's where they went?'

Pietro nodded.

'Yes, now I think of it, it must be. You should try the priest.'

'What's his name?'

'Father Fei. His house is behind the church.'

With that Pietro turned back to work, pumping at the bellows to the furnace, sending a blast of sparks and heat roaring into the workshop.

Sorrel was only too eager to leave.

'Come on,' she said. 'I've had enough of him.'

They scurried back out into the dank morning, but they had found a small rag of hope to hold onto.

'I'm coming, Father,' Marko said to himself. 'I'm coming.'

6

They had to wait a long time for a boat to San Michele. They could see it across the water, halfway back to the city, tantalisingly out of reach. The mist had lifted slightly and weak sunlight shone down on them from time to time, before disappearing behind thicker cloud again.

'If this box they left with had Venetia's tiara in it, why did they take it to San Michele?'

'I don't know,' Sorrel said. 'Maybe it had something else in it. We're just guessing it was the tiara.'

'What else had he been working on?'

Sorrel sighed.

'He'd done no work for months. Not that I know of, anyway. We didn't even know what was wrong to start with. One day I thought Father seemed to be holding his head strangely, as if he had a stiff neck, you know? But when I offered to rub some balm into it, he got angry and said it was nothing. Next day it was worse, and he started knocking into things. He became very clumsy. I thought he was drunk. So did the first doctor who came. And the third, and the fifth. Then he started to sweat, his eyes shrank into their sockets; his pupils were like little black dots. He told me about the curse on our house, though in truth I suppose I had known it all along somehow.

'And then I knew he was dying.'

Marko threw a pebble into the water. They sat on a stone bench by the quay, waiting for someone to leave for San Michele. Had it been Sunday, there might have been a steady stream of traffic for the church, but with little else on the tiny island, and its twin, San Cristoforo, no one was hurrying to get there. Eventually someone would take a boat out, and they could beg a ride, maybe for free, maybe for a song. The only other option was to hire a boatman, and that would cost.

Both Sorrel and Marko were aware that their money was all too exhaustible.

'It must be awful,' Marko said, thinking of Sorrel's father. It was hard to associate her with the black-eyed madman looming behind him in Sorrel's room that morning. Something occurred to him.

77

'Didn't you try that stuff we saw, that they were selling in the city?'

'Teriaca?' Sorrel said, 'Yes, we tried it. And all the idiots who came to the house tried it too. It made no difference. It's supposed to be an antidote to any poison, and yes, it's supposed to bring an easy sleep, and deep. But it never helped my father. You tried it. Well, you smelled it, at least.'

Marko looked at her, a question on his lips, but then he remembered the small blue bottle in her room.

'It's not the worst of it,' she said grimly. 'You read my grandfather's diary. That was while he could still write. Just about. They say the end stages of the death are the worst. It takes for ever. You get more and more desperate for sleep, but it doesn't come. Your heart starts to race, and your eyes shrink to nothing. Then you become paralysed, unable even to speak, but all the time you can still think clearly. Finally your heart gives out. And then you die.'

Marko threw another stone. He had no idea what to say to the sad strange girl whose awful story he had walked into. He wondered whether he'd even chosen to be part of it. Hadn't it been thrust upon him? An unwilling participant. But then, he'd had no choice. He'd wanted to come and find his father, he had to. And his father had had to come and help his old friend. And he'd done that because of some bond of friendship that went back many years, long before Marko was born. It all seemed part of an unbroken chain that probably went back through the pages of time, in which Marko's ancestors lived and died.

78

From there, to here. And now, with Sorrel, waiting for a boat.

'Or maybe they didn't go to San Michele at all.'

'Yes,' Marko said. 'That's possible. But as I said before, we have no other path to follow. If we talk to the priest and he knows nothing, we'll be at a dead end, but at least we've explored the possibility.'

'You're very clever,' Sorrel said suddenly. 'Like your father. Just like him. He would talk like that, explain things. You know?'

'Yes,' said Marko. 'I know.'

And he took some comfort from the fact that though Sorrel might not like him very much, she seemed to have a great respect for his father.

'The diary was very strange in places,' Marko said. 'Do you remember that bit about birds, about geese and feathers? And the last five words. What did that mean?'

'You have to understand that by then he was probably mad half the time. He wouldn't have known what he was writing.'

'Yes,' said Marko. 'I suppose you're right. But it's strange. Odd.'

'I know what strange means.'

I bet you do, thought Marko, but he smiled.

'Yes, I just can't explain myself very well.'

Frustratingly other boats rowed and sailed across the lagoon, and they even saw one land at San Michele, though it had come from another direction. Eventually, they managed to convince a kind fisherman who'd just returned from the lagoon to put out briefly once more to take them the short distance to the island. He rowed steadily across, not asking what they were doing, and

79

paused alongside the jetty just long enough for them to leap ashore. Then he left them.

'How will we get back?' Marko asked.

'Someone will be leaving sooner or later,' Sorrel said. 'That's how it works.'

She didn't sound too certain.

7

It was late afternoon. They had travelled such a short way in truth, but it had taken so long. Marko found that his legs were slightly wobbly from the three boat trips they'd made that day. Sorrel seemed fine and Marko reflected that she, like any other inhabitant of the city, must be used to the constant movement between land and water; an amphibian existence, like that of frogs.

Their destination was obvious.

There was little on the island apart from the church itself. A few single storey houses, some no more than huts, some sturdy enough brick buildings, and a few walls that seemed to denote the boundaries of non-existent properties. The church was out of all proportion to these humble houses, and dwarfed them all, a massive white marble construction, squatting on the island; a leviathan of stone. It seemed likely that the island would at any moment sink under its weight, down into the water.

'Shall we?' Sorrel said, and Marko was already on the way. The place seemed deserted. A small mangy dog ran past them, but otherwise the only life they'd seen was an old woman shrouded from head to foot, working a bucket at a well.

They tried the front of the church, but the door was either stuck, or locked, or simply too heavy for them to move.

'He said round the side, didn't he?' Sorrel said, thinking about the awful Pietro. Why her father had employed him was beyond her, though she knew he'd had little choice.

Around, away from the lagoon-side of the church, they came upon a cluster of buildings that huddled into its protection. They tried the doors, knocking on each, and calling.

'Who's there?' came a voice from inside, and then a black door opened in a whitewashed wall, and a head stuck out. It was obviously the priest.

'Father? Father Fei?' Sorrel asked.

The man nodded. He was middle-aged, very tall, and quite gaunt, with a balding head. His lips were pale, and his skin sallow, but he smiled at them in a friendly way.

'Yes? How can I help you children? Come inside, come inside.'

He ducked back through the doorway and Sorrel and Marko followed. They were in a simple room. A door led off in the direction of the church, and another to rooms leading towards the rest of the village, such as it was. There were two tables in the room. The smaller table was bare but for a couple of dishes and some tiny bottles. Their eyes were drawn to the larger table, which was spread with a decent looking meal, and at the sight of it they both realised how hungry they were.

'How can I help you?' Father Fei repeated.

'We're looking for someone. Two people, really,' Marko said. 'We think they may have come here. About three weeks ago. One of them was Simono Bellini, the glass-maker.'

As he spoke Simono's name, Marko watched the priest's face, hoping for some kind of recognition, but he saw none. Disappointed, he continued.

'He was with another man, about the same age, but taller. Did anyone like that come here? Or to the island itself?'

'I'm sorry, but I don't know. I mean, people come here all the time. Especially on Sundays. Was it a Sunday? I'm afraid then there are many people here.'

'But you'd know a stranger wouldn't you? Your whole congregation can't be so big you wouldn't spot a stranger.'

The priest considered this.

'Yes, you're right. I know everyone.'

'So you don't think you know the men we're looking for?'

The priest smiled.

'No, I don't think I do. Is it important?'

'Very,' Sorrel said, trying to suppress the desperation in her voice.

'I'm sorry,' Father Fei said. 'I hope you find them. Maybe someone else on the island can help. Have you asked anyone else? No? Then you should! But I can see where your eyes are leading you. Would you like some?'

They both tore their eyes from the food on the table, and nodded.

'Yes. Yes please.'

'Excellent. You are always welcome in God's house.' He turned to Marko. 'My friend, would you fetch another chair for yourself, while I help the young lady to some sustenance. There's a spare chair in the bedroom at the end of the corridor.'

Marko did as he was bid, anxious to return before Sorrel had eaten everything. He opened the door to the corridor, and found himself in the dark. He fumbled down and along the passageway until his fingers closed on a door handle, then went in.

This room was slightly lighter, and he saw the chair beside what must be the priest's bed. He entered the room and as he did, smelled a subtle scent that he recognised. He turned in time to flinch as a massive metal hammer swung towards his head. On the other end of the hammer was the swarthy violence of Pietro, his mouth grinning madly with the effort of swinging the weapon.

Marko lifted an arm as he ducked and deflected the full force of the blow, but still the hammer glanced off his head. It seemed like a lifetime went by as he staggered a step forwards, stunned at what had happened, then closed his eyes and sank to the floor. As he blacked out, as if from a great distance, he heard Pietro mutter.

'Now for the pretty one.'

8

Sorrel barely knew what happened. She had just raised a tumbler of water to her lips when the door to the corridor burst open. Expecting to see Marko, she was horrified as Pietro stormed in, wielding a heavy mallet.

'Now I want the rest of my money!' he yelled at her.

She jumped from the chair and stumbled backwards, turning to Father Fei for help, then felt her hope die as she saw him laughing.

'You stupid innocent little girl,' he sneered. 'You'll pay us both twice over for your stupidity.'

She knew she was going to die. Frantically, she made a lunge towards the door, but the priest grabbed her arms and pulled her back against him. She could smell his awful odour, feel his rough hands on her arms, his stubble digging through her hair into her scalp.

'Your boyfriend's dead already, pretty one,' Pietro snarled. 'So there won't be any help from him. Just play nicely, and give us the money and then we'll think what to do with you.'

She knew what they would do with her. And then they would kill her.

She struggled again, harder, and tried to stamp on Fei's foot, but he only held her tighter and bent her arms back so she thought she would faint from the pain.

The door crashed behind her, and she saw the snarl on Pietro's face turn into a mask of surprise.

He pushed past Fei and Sorrel, lifting his hammer. Fei whirled round, throwing Sorrel from him. She fell to the floor, catching her head on the table as she went down, and sank into blackness.

She heard a thin slicing sound, twice, like the wind in the tops of poplar trees, and then nothing else. All was silence, and her eyes closed.

The small mangy dog, with wiry black and grey hair, trotted round the island from house to house, as usual, begging for scraps of food. In a couple of places he was given a morcel of old bread, and in the depths of his dog-mind he could dimly remember the day when someone had given him a huge bone to chew, but today he was hungry. He stopped and drank from a puddle, then trotted on. The night was closing in over the lagoon, and the dog could smell it coming. He lifted his head and waited, and then realised there was something else in the air, another smell. A sweet smell. His nose twitched and pulled him towards the door of the church, which unusually, stood open. That in itself would have been enough of an incentive for him, since he was a curious dog, but it was also where the sweet smell was coming from.

A chill gust of wind slipped across the water and the island, and the dog. He scampered over and squeezed through the narrow gap in the church door. He'd been inside the church once or twice before, but he was nervous. He knew there was a tall man in black who always chased him out, with a kick and a curse, so he went cautiously along the nave, sniffing. The sweet smell seemed to have disappeared, or rather, been masked by the other scents in the church, incense and the tallow of the candles. Then, as he passed a small side door, he picked it up again, and moments later he found a room with a table spread with food. He hopped from chair to table, and began to gnaw at half a cold chicken sitting there.

He was so busy doing this, so hungry, that he didn't stop to think about the girl lying still on the floor, or the two men beside her, or the pooling blood in which they all lay.

10

Sorrel opened her eyes and didn't understand what she saw.

She blinked a couple of times, but the world was definitely wrong. The room she was standing in had turned sideways, and half of it was red. She blinked again and some of the redness got into her eye.

Then she lifted her head slightly, and saw what was next to her, and she screamed.

*   *   *

In the bedroom at the end of the corridor, her screaming found its way slowly into Marko's ears, but from there it was a much longer journey into his mind, clouded and befuddled as it was. Nevertheless, it gradually found its way and woke him from his stupor. He sat up suddenly, bent over and retched from the pain in his head. Gingerly he put a hand up to his left temple, and found a massive lump growing there. He sat for a moment longer, remembered the screaming and lurched down the corridor. As he stood in the doorway, he saw an appalling sight. Sorrel flinched as he came in, then saw who it was, and at least her screaming

86

stopped. She jumped up from where she was and ran to him, burying her head into his side, shaking. Marko stared over her head at where she'd been lying on the floor. On one side of her lay the body of Pietro, a little closer lay the body of the priest. But not quite all of them lay on the floor, for both their heads were missing. The amount of blood covering the floor was both shocking and horrifying, and yet somehow horrendously fascinating. Marko stared at the scene for ages, half in shock, half wondering what had happened. Only after a long while did he realise there was a dog standing on the table, happily eating the food that was supposed to have been for them.

Suddenly, Marko felt he was going to start screaming too, and if he did, he would never stop. He pulled Sorrel down the corridor, still unable to take his eyes off the scene, though as he backed away it shrank in size like a genie in a dream. He got into the priest's bedroom, and pulled Sorrel onto the bed, where they both immediately passed out.

11

When Marko woke again, it was to the sensation of the dog licking his hand. He sat up, and looked at the dog angrily for a moment, then changed his mind. It had nothing to do with any of this. It was lost and hungry, and Marko could do nothing but sympathise. He was half lying on Sorrel, and he got up now, and looked at her. She was an awful mess. The half of her that had been lying on the floor was covered in blood, from head to foot, and that blood was now thickening and drying. She still slept deeply, and Marko was grateful for that.

He looked around the room. It was a simple room, as a priest's room should be, but then, Marko knew that this had been no decent man of God. Who knows what else he was hiding behind the cloth? There was the bed they lay on, the chair he'd been sent to find, a wooden coffer at the foot of the bed, and a large chest of drawers, on the top of which sat a basin and a blue jug. Carefully, he lifted himself off the bed and walked over to the jug. The dog followed eagerly, and as Marko looked inside the jug and saw it was full of water, he felt pity for the animal. He set the basin on the floor and poured a little water into it.

'That's all you can have,' he said. 'We need the rest. So make it last.'

The dog ignored him and began lapping it up furiously.

Marko sat down on the bed beside Sorrel and began to rip small strips from the sheet. These he dipped into the water jug, and then carefully began to wipe the blood away from Sorrel's face.

She stirred gently, but still didn't wake, so he grew bolder and wiped a little harder. For a while he just seemed to make the mess worse, and the blood mixed with her habitual black eye-paint at first, but then he started to see the girl underneath the mess again, and smiled. He looked at her hair and sighed. That would be harder.

He glanced over to the dog and saw it had finished drinking, and was now sitting happily on the floor, its tongue lolling as it gazed at Marko from under comical bushy eyebrows. He took the basin and filled it with water, setting it on the seat of the chair by the bed. Then he lifted Sorrel's shoulders so her hair hung into the bowl, and began to wash it. The clean water was soon pink and then red, but as darkness began to grow in the room, he could no longer see clearly, and he no longer cared.

In the gloom, gazing at her face, gently wiping the water from her brow and neck, he had as much to imagine as to see her face, but he found he could bring it to his mind's eye with ease. His fingers slowed in their task, and he had a rare privilege, to be close to beauty and to be allowed to stare at it without shame. He felt the weight of her head and shoulders in his arms, and sensed her breathing, shallow and disturbed now, and he knew that at that instant, his heart had gone out to her.

She whimpered, like a dreaming dog, and he whispered to her gently.

'It's all right. I'm here.'

At last he thought he had done enough, and he began to lift Sorrel back fully onto the bed. He felt her stirring, and she opened her eyes suddenly, full of panic, and the quietness of moments before evaporated in an instant.

'What are you doing?' she cried. 'Get off me!'

'Sorrel! Sorrel! It's me. Marko. You're all right. We're all right.'

She struggled to sit up and felt her hair.

'What are you doing to me?'

'It's all right now,' he said, trying to soothe her. 'It's all right.'

'Marko!' she said, as if surprised. 'Oh . . .'

She moaned, and he knew she was remembering

everything.

'It's all right,' he said. 'I was just cleaning you up. I . . .'

'They're dead, aren't they?' Sorrel said, interrupting.

He paused.

'Very.'

'What happened?' she cried. 'I thought you were dead. I thought they were going to kill me. And then . . .'

'I don't know. Pietro hit me on the head. When I woke up I came in and found you. And . . . them. And him.'

He turned to point at the dog, and realised it was drinking from the basin.

'Oh, that's disgusting,' he said, 'Stop it!'

He grabbed the basin from the chair and crossing the room, opened a window and threw the water out. The daylight had almost totally gone now and it was hard to see anything in the room itself.

'What are you doing?' Sorrel asked. 'He's just thirsty.'

'The water wasn't . . . clean.'

Sorrel felt her hair again and decided not to ask any more.

'I didn't know what to do about your dress,' Marko said.

'What do you mean?'

'It's . . . not clean, either. I don't think it will wash out, and we don't have much water left.'

Sorrel felt her dress and shuddered, then jumped to her feet and began to drag it off, her fingers scrabbling desperately at the hooks and laces.

90

'Sorrel . . .'

'I'm not staying in it,' she cried, her voice shrill with fear. 'Thank God it's dark in here. God! Take it from me. I don't want it!'

She threw it across the room. Marko could make out her thin arms and legs, and the slightly paler colour of her underclothes. As far as he could see, her thick dress had prevented the blood from staining them.

He stood, and felt like crying at the pitiful mess they were in, but he found that he could not cry, and that it wouldn't help them, so he spoke to Sorrel instead, in what he hoped was a calm voice.

'Get under the blankets. I'm going to have a look around, try and find a light. Then we'll decide what to do.'

He fumbled his way to the chest of drawers. He'd seen there were two shallow drawers at the top, and guessed rightly that one of them must contain candles or a tinderbox.

His hand fell on something even better. There were candles, yes, but he whistled as he took out the strange object from the drawer. He'd only seen one once before, in the house of a rich merchant in Trieste.

'This priest seems to have forgotten the simple life,' he said.

'Why?'

'He owns a tinder pistol. Give me a minute. I've never used one before.'

He set the little hand gun on the top of the chest of drawers and put a candle next to it, ready. He opened the lid of the tinder chamber, a small metal pot where the barrel of the gun should have been. The rest of the gun was still as it had been

91

designed, with a flintlock mechanism. He cocked the pistol, and fired it. There was a flash of sparks, flickering like fireflies in the darkness, and then was gone.

Sorrel shrieked, then sighed.

'You need powder, too.'

'Yes, of course,' said Marko.

He hunted in the drawer, and felt for any secret chambers in the handle of the body of the pistol, but he could find no powder.

'Just have to try without, there may be enough left in the tinder. If we're lucky.'

Five more times he cocked the pistol and fired it. Each time a shower of sparks illuminated the room, then disappeared, plunging them into darkness again. Then, on the sixth attempt, the tinder caught, and a tiny flame licked up into the room long after the sparks had flown.

'Quick!' Sorrel called.

Marko didn't dare answer for fear he'd blow the feeble flame out, but soon had lowered the wick of the candle into its path and the darkness in the room receded a little.

'There's another one. Let me light that too. There.'

With two candles, the room seemed almost cosy.

With more light in the room, Marko suddenly realised that he had missed another chest that stood by the wall. Something about it drew his attention, and he took a candle and went to inspect it. It was a heavy square-topped chest, with a latch, but which appeared to be unlocked. Lifting the lid, his eyes narrowed. Inside was a collection of bottles and phials, which made him remember the others on the table in the dreadful room along the corridor. They were of different sizes and shapes, and contained various liquids and powders. The dishes seemed to have been used for mixing and heating of various contents. He whistled, puzzled now, and turned to find Sorrel next to him.

'What is it?' she asked.

'I . . . don't know,' he said. 'Strange things for a priest to have in his bedroom.'

He picked up one of the bottles and sniffed the stopper, then thrust it away from him in disgust at the horrible odour. He coughed.

'Who knows?' Sorrel said. She shivered.

Marko began to rummage through the rest of the chest of drawers.

'What are you looking for?'

'Something you can wear. You shouldn't get cold.'

'What? Of his?'

'We can't stay here. It's a miracle no one's found us already. Or them. It's our good fortune that this is a miserable little island and no one seems to know, or like the priest. We must have been asleep for hours. But someone will come sooner or later, and then . . .'

'But we didn't do anything.'

'Like you told me . . .'

'Yes, you're right. The last thing we need is any more trouble. But how are we going to get away?'

'Pietro must have come in a boat. The island's not that big. We'll find it and leave while it's dark. But you need something to wear. There's more blankets in here. A bible! I wonder if he ever opened it . . . Wait a minute. What's this?'

Marko's knuckles smarted as they struck something hard in the deep bottom drawer. It was a box, made of wood, about three hands wide and one deep.

'Look,' he said, and brought it over to the candlelight where Sorrel sat shivering under her blanket.

'What is it?' he asked. 'Do you think there's money?'

'Open it and see!'

'It won't. It's locked.'

'Isn't there a key?'

Marko went back to the drawer to look for the key, but found nothing.

'I suppose . . .' he said.

'What?'

'The key might be . . .'

He thought about the body in the other room, and whether he could face going through its pockets.

'Marko!' Sorrel cried. 'Look!'

She held one of the candles right up to the box, and now he saw what he'd missed before. It was a small paper label, pasted in the top left hand corner of the lid. There was a handwritten address on the label, Canareggio 6506, and a name, Nicolo Bruno.

'So?' Marko asked. 'That's where it's going.'

'No, you don't understand. This is my father's writing. This is one of his boxes. It must be the piece they came to collect. And this must be the customer it's for.'

'Then that's where we're going next,' Marko said.

'Yes,' Sorrel said excitedly, 'Yes, but . . .'

The same thought had just crossed Marko's mind.

94

What was the box doing here, in the possession of the foul priest, when it should have been delivered by their two fathers to its new owner? Did that mean it had been taken from them, taken by force? And what if it did?

Marko pushed those thoughts away, and took the box from Sorrel. He shook it gently, and a soft rattling came from inside.

'Careful!'

'Yes,' Marko said.

'What's is in there?'

Marko swallowed hard.

'I'll see if I can find the key,' he said.

12

The city prepared itself for sleep, as night drifted down from the hills and brushed everyone and everything with a touch of the eternal rest that would one day be theirs for good.

All across Venice that weird change that happens once every day was taking place, as somewhere perhaps familiar by daylight becomes foreign, an alien cityscape, of mysterious sights, improbable liaisons and unfulfilled promises. Small boats and larger ones made their way to and fro across the waterways, and as the events of the day made way for the events of the night, many people set out for Giudecca, an infamous place of debauchery and pleasure. Others closed their shutters tight against such wickedness, and prepared to make the long journey through another January night.

In a forgotten corner of the city, an old woman shuffled slowly along. The people she passed paid her no attention, and she both loved and hated this. Oh! She knew what they thought, if they thought of her at all. There goes a senile old hag, no use for anything anymore, too old, too old. She had no strength left, she was weak, and powerless. And how wrong they were! How very wrong they were. Somewhere in an alley behind her lay the body of a strong young man, a body that lay twisted and spent; his death mask a mixture of horror and surprise that recorded the moment of his passing.

Elsewhere, a hopeless gambler strapped on his belt, threw his coat around his shoulders and headed for the Ridotto where he knew his luck was due to change.

A prisoner in the Piombi, the lead-roofed cells in the Doge's palace, scratched at what he thought might be flea bites, then froze as he thought for a moment he heard another scratching from nearby, beyond the wall, as if in answer to his own.

The proprietor of the latest animal attraction to stir the city, a small black rhinoceros, swept away the latest offering of dung, threw fresh straw down for the beast, wondered if it really was looking more ill than the day before, then shrugged and went to count his day's takings.

In the house of the priest at San Michele, nothing happened at all, as the two headless corpses lay in a thick black-red pool of their own making. Even the dog had left now, having sensed the badness of what had happened there.

It trotted out into the night, a misty, damp and cold night, and decided that life could be better than it was. It sniffed the air and picked up a scent, and the scent told him that it was the best thing that had happened to him in a very long while.

He followed it.

Marko and Sorrel hunted around the banks of the island of San Michele, looking for Pietro's boat, and Marko thought to himself for the tenth time how it would probably be best not to make any comment about the makeshift clothes Sorrel was wearing. They'd found some trousers and a nightshirt that must have belonged to Fei, and deciding that he no longer needed them, Sorrel had tried them on. The trousers were ridiculously long; the priest had been a tall man, and even rolling them up had helped little. In the end Marko had used a knife to hack the bottoms from them, and Sorrel had pulled the huge nightshirt over her head and tied it around the waist with a belt made from a strip of cloth. The linen was old and stiff, and Sorrel looked terrible, but there was nothing else to do. Still, she refused to leave her dress, which she carried rolled up under one arm.

As they were hunting for the boat in the darkness, edging their way with a candle as light, daring to use no more, they suddenly heard a scuffling noise. They both stopped instinctively, and scanned the mist for the source of the sound. Sorrel laughed. The little stray trotted into view and right up to Marko, where he sat, looking up expectantly at what he had decided was his new master.

Sorrel laughed again.

*　　　*　　　*

In a short skiff in the middle of the Northern lagoon, the tall old man in black bent over his oars and drifted for a while. He was as far from land as he'd be for the whole journey, and bending under the thwart he pulled out something long and thin. In the lightless gloom of night on the lagoon, what he held was indistinct, a harmless looking object about three feet long, like a stick, or a baton of some sort. But the old man, who had nearly forgotten that his name was Peter, knew exactly what it was. He rummaged around by his feet once again and found a scrap of rag. Then, very, very carefully, almost lovingly, he wiped the drying blood from the curved blade of the Turkish sword, as if wiping a baby's mouth after a messy feed.

When he was done, he threw the rag overboard, and slid the sword back into its leather scabbard. Once upon a time there had been no scabbard, just a long wooden box, but as the distances he travelled had become greater, and the need to travel light had grown greater too, he'd had a tanner in Reval make the sheath for him. It was perfect in its own way, though even this scabbard was very old now, and showed signs of the years and the miles it had covered. Peter had had the tanner emboss the faces of the leather with various patterns and markings, and had been insistent as he'd instructed the man to inscribe a name at the scabbard's mouth. The leather was old and worn now, and the name had been rubbed countless times by Peter's hand as he grasped the sheath in his left hand, pulling the sword itself with his right. It was hard to read anymore, and Peter himself had nearly forgotten it, but a close inspection

might have yielded the name, a girl's name.
It might have been Sophia.

A Fairy Tale

It was no use.

Though everyone tried to persuade the King to change his mind, he would not be swayed.

'If I don't stick to the rules that I make,' he said, 'how can I expect my subjects to obey them?'

And with that, the pair, the princess and the beggar, were married, and more than that, the King was so angry with the girl that he sent them away that very night, banishing her from the castle for ever.

The beggar was very pleased with his good fortune, and though he was poor, he was not so old, and even a little handsome. He thanked Fate for steering his course. The princess's sisters took pity on her, and begged their new husbands for a little money to give the poor couple before they left, but though the men were rich, they were jealous of their wealth, and would only spare a few coins to send the princess and the beggar on their way.

The princess was distraught, but the beggar was happier than ever. It was more money than he'd ever had in his life, and with it he bought a small hovel, deep in the woods, and an axe.

The couple set up house, and for a while, things were miserable for the princess, and wonderful for the beggar. He used the axe to cut down trees, and began to make money selling the firewood. His wife was young and beautiful, and life was good, and amazingly enough, as the years rolled by, the haughty princess cried so many tears, that she washed all the pain out of her heart. She looked up one spring day to see her husband coming home with a bag of coins in one hand, and a rabbit for the pot in the other, and she realised with a shock that she loved him.

THREE

1

In a deathly hush she moved on the water.

There was no stopping her, for she was the air one moment, water the next, fire if that was what was needed. She approached without warning, as she had done so many times, moving here, moving there, bringing with her her own variety of evil.

She was death. She could be life too, but only rarely. Her face was the face of abject horror, of abandonment, of defeat, of resignation to the inevitable. One breath from her could take all breath from her victim, and she looked forward to doing that again, and again and again.

She felt all her years gathered about her like an army, countless centuries of the evil she'd done sweeping round her like plague rats on a doomed ship.

She'd been so many places, lived in so many hearts turned bad, and won so many victories, and she didn't intend for it to end. Ever.

A smile appeared on her face, her wide thin mouth like a slit in a bag of white flour, opening and closing like a trap for beetles to stray into, her nose like an eagle's beak jutting over it, her black eyes, in truth quite elegant, radiating all manner of devilment and destruction.

She thought of all the names, everything that anyone had ever cursed her with, had ever whispered in horror, and yet, in all the years, there was still one that suited her best, the one they used in the forests in the east.

The Shadow Queen.

She laughed, and as she did so, small creatures withered and died.

2

Now, Marko and Sorrel, and their new companion, drifted in open water, bobbing slightly on the swell, though it was a lifeless night on the lagoon.

It had not been easy to find Pietro's boat. They'd started their search close to the church where it stood by the water's edge, but in the end hunted right round the small island's banks and shores without success. Finally, as they approached the church again after making a complete circuit of San Michele, Marko saw a tiny cut in the bank they'd not seen before. It was almost invisible from the direction they'd started from, and even in daylight would have been hard to see. On their way round the island they'd tiptoed past houses with candlelight inside, and the muffled sounds of domestic life. Once a door had opened, and they'd frozen like statues until it closed again, Marko's heart in his mouth as the dog had cocked its head towards the sound, perhaps imagining it was a sign of the arrival of food. But the dog had remained quiet enough, and had not given them away.

'Is this the sort of company you usually keep?' Sorrel had asked, teasing Marko about the dog. He'd ignored her, though he was pleased to hear her say something. She'd barely spoken a word since she'd donned the terrible clothes. It wasn't just that they were a man's clothes, ill-fitting and dirty. There was something awful knowing they

106

belonged to a dead man, and one who'd tried to kill them at that. Marko shuddered at the thought of it, and determined to get Sorrel back into her own dress as soon as it was possible.

*   *   *

They sat in the boat, exhausted, their thoughts mixed and troubled. Even the dog seemed to sense the mood, and lay in the bottom of the craft, his chin resting on Marko's foot.

Between them sat the box. Marko had not been able to find the key, though it was possible he'd missed it. It had not been a pleasant job. In his work for his father, he was used to seeing wounds and sores, festering cuts and disfiguring illnesses, and even the occasional basic surgical exploration inside a human body, but nothing could have prepared him for his second visit to the room where Fei and Pietro, or what was left of them, lay. Without heads, without their faces, it was hard to think of them as men at all, just grotesque lumps of meat, bone and fat. That was all they were now, he decided, and tried to detach himself from what he had to do. If only there hadn't been quite so much blood. He'd approached the bodies cautiously, as if they might leap back to life at any moment. He'd tried Fei's robes first, feeling inside the priest's habit for any pockets, chains or purses. He'd found nothing, and almost with relief had moved onto Pietro. Unlike Fei, who'd been lying on his back, the glass-maker's man was prone, chest to the floor, and Marko realised he would have to turn him over to reach into his pockets.

He swallowed hard, put a hand on Pietro's

shoulder, and began to pull. There was an awful sweet smell and a sucking sound and then Marko noticed something else, a mark on the back of the glass-man's neck, beneath the frighteningly smooth cut which had severed his life from his body. That was enough for Marko, and suppressing the urge to be sick, he dropped the shoulder back to the floor. As he left, however, a desire for knowledge, stronger than his disgust, overcame him. Something nagged at him, and making his way back to Fei, he'd lifted and rolled him with a foot, so that he too lay chest down. There on his neck, was the same mark.

Marko had fled as if the devil was behind him.

3

'What do we think happened?' Marko lifted his head and the dog stirred. He vaguely noticed that Sorrel had said 'we', not 'you', and for some reason he couldn't quite place it gave him a little hope. They'd brought some blankets from the priest's room, and huddled under them in the small boat.

'Do you mean . . . to those two? Who killed them? Why we weren't killed too?'

Sorrel nodded. 'No. Well. Yes, that too. It's an extraordinary thing.'

Marko smiled to himself. That's not the way he would have described it, but then Sorrel always seemed to have an unusual view of things.

'I meant what happened to our fathers. What really happened out there. On Murano, on San Michele.'

Marko thought for a while, and though he'd been running all sorts of ideas back and forth through his mind all night, the cold was affecting him so badly that he struggled to put these thoughts in any kind of order.

'Your father made . . . something. For someone. And it's whatever's in that box. Agreed?'

Sorrel nodded, too tired and cold to tell Marko how obvious he was being.

'We don't know what it is. Maybe it's Venetia's tiara. But then why would it be addressed to this man, Nicolo Bruno? And you're sure it's your father's writing?'

Sorrel nodded again.

'Yes, I think so.'

'You think so?'

'I know so. It's just a bit shaky. Uneven.'

Marko thought to himself that it was amazing that Simono Bellini could write at all, given the mad wretch of a man he'd met the night before. But on the day that he and Alessandro had made the trip, Bellini had been better. Maybe not utterly well, but much, much better than he had been.

'All right. So let's assume it's not Venetia's tiara, but something for someone else. Something for Nicolo Bruno. My father and your father went to collect it from the workshop, to take it to Bruno, to sell it to him. But it never got there. Somewhere it went missing, Pietro or Fei, or both of them, must have stolen it from them.'

'In which case . . .'

Sorrel stopped. The conclusion was obvious. In all likelihood, Marko's father had never left Murano. Not alive, at least. Maybe he was already drifting towards the bottom of the lagoon somewhere.

Marko shook his head.

'But listen. Where was your father found? Not on Murano?'

Sorrel understood.

'No. No, he was found wandering around San Marco. Back in the city. Then they brought him home.'

'So if he got back as far as the city, that means that my father probably did too. That whatever happened to them happened there, and not on Murano, or San Michele.'

Sorrel hesitated, but she could not stop herself from expressing her fears.

'Does it?'

Marko ignored this. It was something he could not afford to ponder too deeply.

'Assume they made it back to the city, but they never made it to Bruno. Fei and Pietro follow them, and fight them, steal the box, take it out to San Michele. Pietro only sent us there as a trap, I don't think our fathers were ever there at all.'

'No,' Sorrel agreed. 'Maybe not. In fact, I think you're right. But where does that get us? Where do we go now?'

'We go to Bruno. We deliver the goods to him, as arranged.'

'And why do we do that?'

'Two reasons. We could use the money. And more importantly, he might just know something. When they were supposed to come. Who they spoke to. Something.'

Sorrel didn't reply but her silence was enough to anger Marko.

'What else are we going to do, Sorrel?' he asked

bitterly. 'What else?'

She hung her head and Marko knew that was as much agreement as he'd get.

He looked away from her and across the water to the light of the city.

Somewhere, in some room of some house in the city, his father was still alive. He couldn't let himself think otherwise.

4

They spent the rest of the night moored to a huge wooden post that reared from the lagoon some way off shore, and only as day broke did they head in for the banks of the city. It was another grey and cloudy day, and as they drew into the fondamente the buildings seemed more ghostly than ever, rising out of the water like painted drops in a theatre, flat and pale.

They were frozen stiff after their night in the boat, but as Marko began to row, he started to feel his blood warm him again. He looked across at Sorrel. Without her eye paint, in the early morning light, she no longer looked angry and bitter-tongued. She looked tired and lonely, but lovely too, as she tickled Dog under his chin, feeling his warmth on her fingertips.

'Head up that way,' she suggested. 'It will be quieter there, past that basin. It's a little harbour. Beyond are fishing houses and washing houses.'

Marko bent to the oars and did as he was told, and very soon they chose an obscure jetty to moor alongside.

'What about the boat?' Marko asked.

'We're not stopping here,' Sorrel said. 'We'll go on to Bruno's house in it, as far as we can. But I want to try something first.'

Marko watched as Sorrel walked quickly away across the pavement that led to the first houses, lower and much more modest affairs than the grand palazzo in the heart of the city by the Canalazzo. Even though it was only just light, Sorrel had seen that the washerwomen were already at their work, scrubbing clothes in the great stone basins designed for the purpose, hanging them out on lines to dry. The washing lines were strung from building to building like sails, Marko thought, making them look like huge sea-faring vessels. Sorrel was talking to a washerwoman who stood pinning wet clothes over the washing lines. Marko doubted that they would dry quickly, if at all, in the damp cold weather, but while he was thinking about this he saw Sorrel pointing and the woman nodding back at her. She disappeared inside a house for a while but came back out with some things bundled in her arms. Sorrel picked at the bundles, then seemed to agree something, and then Marko saw her hand her blood-stained dress to the washerwoman. Then both of them vanished inside the house, and a minute later Sorrel reappeared wearing a simple red dress, close to a perfect fit. She came back to the boat, and smiled.

'It's not great, but it will have to do.'

'What did you say?'

'I swapped my dress for this. Mine's worth much more, even in the state it's in. She was happy to give me this one for it.'

Marko looked at her, and couldn't see the problem. It was a deep red colour, not silk, but linen, and in his eyes suited her well. It just swept the ground, and had a high waist that pulled in tight, making her look as shapely as a woman ten years older.

'I don't see what's wrong with it,' he said, genuinely.

Sorrel pulled a face.

'Well, it's not black, for a start,' she said, but she smiled.

Marko laughed.

'We can always dye it later,' he said. 'Come on. How do we find this house?'

'In the boat. The house numbers are sometimes a little hard to follow, and I don't know this area of the city very well.'

They climbed back into the boat, and Sorrel inspected the label on the box.

'5696,' she said. I think that's more likely to be back towards the centre, towards the Canalazzo. We'll try this canal here.'

She pointed to a canal that led straight into the heart of the city. It was reasonably wide, wide enough for two large boats to pass each other comfortably, and travelled dead straight until the mist hid it from view.

'We can ask as we go. If we find any houses between 5000 and 6000 we'll know we're getting near. It usually works.'

'Usually?'

'Usually.'

Marko untied the rope from the jetty, and was starting to pull away when Sorrel laughed.

'Aren't you forgetting someone?'

113

Marko looked and saw the dog was still on the pavement, ferreting around for a scent. Suddenly it heard a squeak of an oar, saw that they were leaving, and ran for the jetty, hopping into the boat with a spring that didn't seem to trouble it at all.

Immediately, it took up its position at Marko's feet, but with its head raised and looking eagerly over the side, trying to see where they were going.

'Don't you think it's about time you introduced us?' Sorrel said, smiling.

Marko didn't smile, but bent his back to the rowing.

'I don't know what he's called,' he said.

'Then perhaps he needs a new name. To start his new life.'

'His new life?'

'With you.'

'Maybe. But I still don't know his name.'

'Then you should give him a name, Marko. You owe him that at least.'

'I do?' Marko said. 'All right. I'll give him a name. I'll call him Dog.'

'Dog? You can't call him Dog!'

'Why not?'

'I could have given him a better name than that.'

'But you said it was up to me to name him, so there you are. His name's Dog. Dog, this is Sorrel. Sorrel, this is Dog.'

'Well!' Sorrel snorted. She glared at Marko, then stared over the side of the boat into the mist. 'What sort of a name is that?'

Marko pulled on the oars and grinned to himself, then grinned down at Dog, who looked back at him, panting, apparently very happy with his new name.

114

They left the boat far behind, and Marko was glad of it. He resisted the temptation to say 'back on firm ground' because to him nowhere in Venice felt like firm ground. It was impossible to forget for a moment that the whole city rested on the unstable muds of a marshy lagoon, even the pavements frequently rang hollow under their feet, witness to the drains and other hidden channels that lurked beneath.

He found himself swaying as they set off on foot, his body having spent so long trying to accustom itself to the swaying of life on the water that it refused to behave now they were on dry land.

Sorrel had no such problems, but Marko reasoned that she would have grown used to this amphibious routine, switching from water to land a dozen times a day.

'6105,' Sorrel said, and pointed to a number on a house nearby. Not every house had one, but most seemed to; one brick was painted white and edged with black; the number elegantly but boldly painted in black inside.

They came to a sort of crossroads, one arm of which led over a small wooden bridge, the others led straight into more alleyways.

'There,' Sorrel said. '6072. We'll try that way.'

She seemed to be right, as the numbers began to fall consistently.

Marko, who was carrying the box, checked the number again. 5696.

The sun poked its feeble face out from the grey sky, and things seemed to be going well, but then Sorrel stopped. The numbers continued to fall as they crossed a couple of small alleys, but then began to climb again.

'We'll have to go back,' she said, but didn't sound concerned, though Marko began to wonder how anyone found their way anywhere in this labyrinth.

'Here?' Marko suggested.

'Here,' Sorrel said, and set off again, with Marko and Dog obediently following. Marko knew there was no sense in interfering; this was her territory. Sure enough, the numbers began to fall again, until they found themselves at 5712.

Sorrel stopped again.

'Now what?' Marko asked, looking ahead. 'Look. There's 5710.'

'I know,' Sorrel said sharply. 'But we're not going that way.'

'Why not?'

'Because I know where we are, and I won't go that way.'

She nodded ahead, refusing even, it seemed, to lift her hand towards the route ahead.

Marko began to feel frustration rising up in him.

'And why won't you go that way? It looks easy enough.'

'Because there are stories about this place,' she said. 'And I won't go there.'

Marko put the box down and turned Sorrel by the shoulders to face him.

'Stories?' he said. '*Stories?* I didn't think you were supposed to believe in stories and superstitions.'

Sorrel pulled back out of his grasp angrily.

'This is Venice,' she whispered, almost as if the houses might overhear her, 'and you don't know anything. You see that house there?'

She pointed, but said nothing.

'Yes,' said Marko, following her brief gesture with puzzlement, wondering what was so special about a house that seemed more or less like all the others in the row.

'Oh!' she said. 'Never mind.'

With that, she picked up the box, and set off the way they had come, then turned the corner of the street.

'Sorrel! Wait!'

Marko rounded the corner and found Sorrel waiting for him impatiently.

'What?' he said. 'I didn't say anything!'

'You didn't need to. I know what you're thinking.'

'Do you?' Marko asked. 'Why not try me? Listen. Tell me what's wrong. I promise I'm listening. If something is so bad that it's scaring you then I'm more than happy to go another way. But please let's just do it quickly.'

Sorrel's shoulders dropped and she sighed.

'I'm just being foolish, I suppose,' she said. 'I'm sorry. I shouldn't be scared, but there are all sorts of stories from that house, that street.'

'What sort of stories?'

'Lots of them. But that house. They say a magician used to live there. My father told me, too, so it must be true. He was an awful man, so the stories say. A brutal, terrible man with no fear of life or death or anyone or anything. They say he'd made a pact with the devil, more than once.'

She paused and Marko could see she was truly frightened by her own story. He let her continue.

'He was coming home late one night, past the cemetery, and suddenly a thick mist fell around him, and he couldn't see to put one foot in front of the other. So he called out to the devil. "Lucifer! Lucifer!" he said. "Throw me a torch to light my way." And immediately a burning torch appeared in his hand and with it he made his way home. It was only when he got there that he saw what he'd been holding. It was the hand of a dead man, and each of the fingers was alight.'

Marko swallowed.

'What did he do?'

'He laughed! This wasn't the first time the devil had played a trick on him in some way or other. He blew the torch out, put it in his log basket, and went to sleep. The next night, when there was no mist, he took it back to the cemetery and gave it back to the dead man who it belonged to, who thanked him and went back into his grave.'

She stopped, and despite the strengthening sunlight, Marko shivered. Something reminded him of the markings he'd seen on the back of Fei and Pietro's necks, marks that he had since realised were tattoos. He wondered whether to tell Sorrel what he'd seen, but decided against it. Suddenly, the certainties of life in his father's surgery in Piran seemed very far away. He'd been brought up to trust only what his eyes saw; his father spent hours when Marko was a child, teaching him, showing him the way the world seemed to him. He could clearly remember his father letting a bee sting his own hand, and hold it under a microscope so Marko could watch the action of the sting as it pumped its poison into the skin. His father had ignored the pain, just so he could explain what was happening to the little Marko. Marko had watched wide-eyed, half in wonder, half in fear for his father, until with the back of his nail Alessandro had scraped the sting away, then set about mixing a small concoction.

'Vinegar and a little *saleratus*,' he'd told Marko. 'That will destroy the poison. The pain will subside soon.'

His father was a remarkable man, who had even confided to Marko that he thought there was no such thing as God, though swearing him to secrecy on the matter.

'Only trust what your eyes tell you, Marko,' he'd told him, adding hastily. 'But tell no one I told you this. I would be in a lot of trouble. The church would try and execute me. And what your mother would do would be worse.'

But in Venice, things didn't seem to follow the same rules, and Marko had begun to doubt that he could always know what was right and what was false. Maybe it wasn't always possible to trust what your eyes told you.

He looked around the empty streets, and finally back at Sorrel.

'Let's go another way, shall we?' he said.

6

'Are you hungry?' Sorrel said.

'Are you joking?'

She shook her head. They'd taken a detour as

119

Sorrel had demanded but it was taking a long time. Once or twice Marko even suspected they were lost, but he didn't say so to Sorrel. It was mid-morning and the day was as bright as it was probably going to get.

'I'm ravenous,' Sorrel said. 'We'll be there soon, but there's a water-shop around the corner. We can buy something to eat. Have some coffee. Do you like coffee?'

'A little,' Marko lied. He'd never drunk coffee in his life. He knew it was a sophisticated drink from the city, and that his father often moaned about not getting any in Piran, but that was all. But he wasn't going to let Sorrel know that.

'Well, come on then.'

Dog trotted after them as they turned the corner and ducked under the low doorway of the water-shop. There were no other customers, and it was dim and cosy, a pleasant change from the chill day outside. The shop sold a lot more than water, Marko soon saw. Drinks of all sorts; lemon water, juice from oranges, chocolate, various kinds of coffee, and wine from all over the Veneto.

'What kind of coffee do you like?' Sorrel asked, approaching the counter. A kind-looking old woman stood waiting for them to order.

'I'll have what you're having,' Marko said quickly. 'And can we get some water for Dog?'

Sorrel laughed.

'He can drink at the fountain in the street like any other cur. We passed one just outside.'

Marko took Dog by the black fur at his neck and shoved his nose towards the small fountain that poured a continuous stream of water out of a small carved lion's mouth set into the wall of the street.

120

Dog however, was having none of it and as soon as he went back inside, he immediately followed.

'There's no getting rid of you, is there?' Marko sighed. 'Well, if you go thirsty it's your own fault.'

He was ducking under the doorway when his attention was caught by three figures coming down the street. He guessed from their clothes and their gait that they were all men, but the masks they wore completely covered their faces. The three were loud and raucous and something about them made Marko step back inside the shop quickly. They went past, shouting and pushing at one another; if it hadn't been so early Marko would have guessed they were drunk. Their masks were unlike any he'd seen so far; many people wore either a mask with a huge bird's beak, or a plain white mask that more or less copied the human face, but which jutted out from the top lip, to enable the wearer to sip at a drink without removing it. The masks that these three wore were altogether different; they were painted red and black, scowling, fiendish things that made the men look like devils.

'Why do people wear those?' Marko asked, sitting down next to Sorrel. Dog curled up at his feet and the woman trudged over with two cups and a steaming pot of coffee.

'It's Carnival,' Sorrel said. 'Anyone can wear a mask during the carnival.'

'But why?'

Sorrel shrugged.

'It's what we do. Just because we can. Maybe to hide, or to pretend you're someone else. Anyone can wear a mask, rich or poor, nobleman or peasant. Under the mask, people become more or

121

less the same. You could have affairs with your lovers and go unrecognised. Eavesdrop, find out what is being said about you, to spy on others . . . The Three, the Inquisitors, make much use of them, I'm sure. But only during Carnival. To wear a mask outside of Carnival is a terrible crime. It is punishable. With whipping, and prison.'

'They send you to prison for wearing a mask?'

'For two years, if you're a woman. Longer for a man.'

Marko shook his head.

'That's crazy.'

'There's a saying here; "Respect Venice". It's not wise to ignore it.'

'I won't forget.'

'Good. Drink your coffee.'

Marko gingerly lifted the cup to his mouth. It smelled bitter, but quite nice, he thought, though too hot to drink. He put the cup down. Sorrel sipped at hers, unconcerned.

'And the carnival? What happens then?'

'Everything happens then. By night mostly, but there's going to be the procession of the new Doge. That's tomorrow afternoon, but it'll go on late. Very late. That's what Venetia wants her tiara for . . .'

'Don't worry about her,' Marko said.

'I won't. We've more important things to worry about. But it's the high point of the carnival. The whole city will don masks, more or less. And there'll be the Flight of the Turk, too. That's wonderful. It's my favourite thing. I can remember the very first time I saw it after we'd moved from London. You won't believe it.'

Sorrel stopped, realising she'd got carried away,

and had for a moment, forgotten the predicament they were in. The truth that her father was mad and dying, that Marko's father was missing. But Marko saw that for a moment, she'd been happy. Really happy, he'd seen her whole face change, relax, become lighter, and prettier, like she'd looked the previous night as he'd washed her hair while she slept. He encouraged her to go on.

'Tell me about it,' he said. 'It sounds fun. Who's the Turk?'

'Well, he's not a Turk. Not any more. It can be anyone, someone different every year, sometimes more than one man. They fix a rope, right up in the sky, from the bell tower of San Marco to the balcony of the Doge's palace. Sometimes they even run the rope out to sea to a ship anchored in the lagoon. Then a man will walk the rope, like at the circus. Have you ever been to a circus, Marko?'

'They come to our town sometimes,' Marko said. 'You mean the man who walks on a rope? He walks right across the square and out to sea? That's impossible!'

'It's dangerous, but not impossible. Many men have died trying it. That's why people come. Like an execution.'

Marko sensed she was sailing back into gloomy waters and tried to steer her out.

'But the rope, it must swing about.'

'Yes, terribly. But it's a very thick rope, about half as wide as your foot, very heavy. So they just swing with it. And most of the time they make it. You're not drinking your coffee and we should pay and get going.'

Marko knew she was right, and picked up his cup, nervously.

'Lovely,' he said, and took a long drink.

Immediately he felt terrible. It felt as if thick black acid was pouring down inside him, and almost straight away his heart began to thump in his chest. Trying to hide it, he couldn't help but pull a face. He opened his mouth to speak but couldn't.

'Yes,' Sorrel said, standing up to leave. 'You're right, it's not very good. But they don't always get the best stuff.'

She made her way to the counter to pay, and Marko let his forehead sink onto the table, panting for breath. Dog looked up at him, cocked his head to one side, and then began to lick his hand.

'It's all right, Dog,' Marko gasped. 'I really think I'll be all right.'

7

Canareggio 5696. They stood in front of the door, listening to the tinkling of a bell die away.

Marko let his hand fall from the bell pull, and turned to Sorrel. 'Trust what your eyes tell you,' his father would say, but why was it that he was filled with a terrible sense of dread about this place? It was still the only choice they had, the only path to follow, but now that they were actually here, something seemed wrong.

It was hard to explain. They were back in the heart of the city, and the buildings were fine and grand. 5696 was perhaps not the largest house, but it looked a well kept merchant's house, or similar, and generally prosperous, from the varnished front door to the shiny brass bell pull, cold to Marko's touch.

He opened his mouth to say something, but Sorrel beat him to it.

'I know. But what else are we going to do? I'm sure Bruno is a reasonable man if he's one of my father's customers.'

Marko nodded, trying to look confident. He held the mysterious box tightly, tighter than he needed to.

'How shall we do this?' he asked, but Sorrel never answered, because a face appeared in a tiny window by the door. It glanced at them, then disappeared. There was a muffled call and the door swung open.

A short, thin man, with a miserable look stood before them. He kept one hand on the door as if he might slam it shut in an instant. His eyes were as thin as his fingers, and not only was he short, he stooped terribly from age. Behind him another indistinct figure scurried away into the bowels of the house.

'Yes?'

Marko tried to sound more composed than he was.

'We've come to deliver this to Signor Bruno,' he said, and indicated the box.

The man said nothing. He seemed unimpressed.

'Very well. You'd better come in. I'll see if the master is free to receive you.'

They followed the old servant into the house, and he shut the door behind them. It closed with a heavy thud and both Marko and Sorrel felt their fears flutter inside them.

'Wait in there,' the man said, pointing to a room

straight ahead of them, while he turned and made his way up a broad staircase that wound out of sight to the first floor.

They did as they were told and found themselves in a formal reception room, which spanned the width of the house. It was dimly lit, but they could see well enough that it was an imposing room. The floors were polished wood, and the walls were hung with an ornate printed paper, luscious red-gold foliage on a midnight blue backdrop. There were paintings, mostly scenes from the Bible; a Madonna and child, the martyrdom of San Sebastian with his arrows holding him to a withered tree, Lazarus rising from his grave. There was little else in the room but at one end was a dais, a small raised platform, and on this stood a large and heavy chair, practically a throne given its size and magnificence. Marko and Sorrel both had the same thought at once. Whoever sat in this chair was used to being obeyed. Dog whimpered slightly and hung close to Marko's legs.

A voice cut towards them through the darkness. 'Who comes?'

A man entered the room, a creature. A thing. He walked slowly, but steadily he made his entrance. He was enormously fat. Marko had never seen anyone so large in all his life, and he had to struggle not to stare as the man dragged one foot after the other in his approach to the chair on the platform. He was finely dressed, in a rich coat and wig, and well-made shoes of red leather. He had reached the dais and Marko and Sorrel could do nothing but watch this vast figure lift one foot then the other the few inches up onto

126

the platform. It required vast effort and for a while it looked touch and go as to whether he would make it at all, but he won this battle and took four more tiny steps before turning and collapsing on the throne.

He closed his eyes. No one spoke. Then his eyes flicked open again, Sorrel wished they had stayed shut. They were hideous slimy yellow things that poured hate out into the room, yellow like a weeping sore, with black dots for pupils, and the only mercy was that they were largely hidden by the drooping folds of eyelid. His whole face drooped in the same way, like some bag of flesh from the butcher's market, it sagged, quivered and twitched at the slightest movement, as if there were rats moving beneath the bloated, blotched skin.

He spoke. His voice was thick and cluttered, and for some reason Marko was reminded of the corpses he'd occasionally seen on his father's surgery table.

'I think, that that is for me.'

His eyes speared the box.

'But who are you?'

The voice roared and the flesh quivered; the rats scurried around inside the face.

'I am Nicolo Bruno!'

Sorrel faltered.

'I'm sorry.'

'Sorry?' he roared, but then lost interest. His eyes crawled back to the box once more.

'I think I asked you a question. Doesn't that belong to me?'

Sorrel felt her fear grow even wilder. She felt there was something not being said, and it was something bad.

Bruno laughed.

'Do you not know who I am? I am Nicolo Bruno, and I am one of the Three Inquisitors of Venice. And you are in a lot of trouble.'

He laughed again, and Dog began to whimper.

8

'Why have you come here? Bruno leaned forward slightly in his chair, peering at them through slits.

'We've brought this for you,' Marko stammered. 'We have come to collect payment for it.'

Sorrel spoke hurriedly.

'My father made it for you but it was never delivered. We want to know if you have seen my father.'

Bruno ignored her.

'Is that it?' he drawled.

'Yes,' said Marko. The box felt like lead in his hands.

'Come closer,' Bruno ordered. 'I want to see it.'

Unwillingly, Sorrel and Marko stepped closer to the platform.

Bruno sneered.

'Your father is Simono Bellini, yes?'

Sorrel nodded quickly.

'Simono Bellini,' Bruno said, his voice sprawling over the name with such distain and distaste that Sorrel would never forget it. He spoke her father's name as though it was an insult.

'And you want to deliver this to me? Yes?'

'That's right,' Marko said.

'You would swear to that in a court?'

Sorrel hesitated, Marko opened his mouth but closed it again.

'You would *swear* it?' Bruno roared and Marko was so startled he stammered back an answer.

'Yes. We want to be paid for it.'

'So,' Bruno said, and here, he slowly and deliberately pulled himself to his feet, pointing a short fat finger at them. 'You want to deliver this to me, and you expect to be paid for it. But tell me, why would I want to pay for something that has already been delivered to me once, and for which I have already paid?'

His words floated into the silence of the room and died. Marko cursed quietly. It was worse than they might have thought, much worse.

'So, it seems I have a pair of thieves before me. A pair of urchins who dare to sell back to me what is already mine. Such stupidity! Such gall! But that is what you are! Thieves!'

'No!' Marko cried, 'It's not like that. We found the box, and we thought it hadn't been given to you yet . . .'

Bruno shouted over their heads.

'Beppe! Call the men!'

'No! Wait! We found it. We'll give it back to you. We'll just give it back and go.'

'And where did you "just find" the box?' Bruno sneered.

'We found it on San Michele,' Sorrel spluttered. 'There were two men.'

'Who?'

'A priest and a glass-maker.'

'And they gave you the box?'

'No, not exactly.'

129

'Beppe!' Bruno screamed, his whole face wobbling from side to side with the effort. He stepped off the platform towards Marko and Sorrel, who stepped backwards defensively. Dog scrabbled to his feet and began to circle Marko's legs. Bruno heaved himself towards them.

'And these men can vouch for what you are saying?'

'No, no they can't,' Marko said uneasily.

'Why not?'

'Because they're dead.'

'What! Dead!'

'Someone killed them,' Sorrel explained.

'Not you?' Bruno sneered. 'Someone?'

Marko and Sorrel started to back away to the door, and then Dog snarled and they turned to see what he was snarling at.

There in the door were the three masked figures they'd seen pass the water-shop.

'At last!' roared Bruno. 'Take these two away and lock them in the strong room.'

'Run Sorrel!' Marko yelled. 'Run!'

She'd already had the same idea, and they both sprinted towards the door, trying to dodge past the three men. Sorrel managed to miss the first hand that grasped for her, and made it to the hallway with Dog running at her heels, but Marko, still clinging onto the box, was caught straight away by the largest figure. He felt arms tighten around his waist and saw the third man coming towards him. He wrestled his arms free and threw the box at this man as hard as he could manage.

As he did so, two things happened simultaneously; Nicolo let out an ugly cry of despair, and the man Marko had thrown the box at

130

deftly caught it, and then gently put it on the floor, before turning back to Marko with a snarl loud enough to hear from under his mask.

'Well done!' cried Nicolo.

Sorrel turned as she ran, and saw Marko was caught.

'Run!' he gasped at her, and as she turned back towards the door, she ran straight into the withered old man who'd let them in. They both went flying to the floor, and moments later the first of the men was on her, yanking her by her hair onto her back, standing over her. He reached down and slapped her across the face.

Marko yelled something, but it was too late. The man who'd caught the box leered at him, and while his partner held Marko tight, he swung a hard fist into his stomach.

Marko slumped over, and in his daze saw Dog running madly around the hall, unsure what to do. Marko mustered all his energy to scream at him.

'Run!'

Dog did as he was told. It was pointless, but somehow there was a tiny sense of delight in the fact that Dog skipped through the hall, right through the old man's legs, who swung at him with a boot. Dog took one leap onto a chair that stood by the wall, and then scrambled through the open window next to the front door.

Marko lifted his head, trying to see Sorrel, and his skin crawled. Her assailant stood over her, dragging her to her feet, but as he did so, Marko caught a glimpse of the back of his neck. There it was again. That strange tattoo.

Subdued, and beaten, Marko and Sorrel were hauled back in front of Bruno. His chest heaved as

131

if he'd exerted himself in the fight, when all he'd done was watch happily as his men got the better of the two.

'As I said.'

He paused for breath, then his slug of a voice crawled over their faces again.

'As I said. Take these two and lock them up. As it happens I have already today received an accusation from the Mouth of Truth, denouncing the girl's father. It seems they are as thick as thieves. I will decide what is to be done with them later, but they are to be arrested on the suspicion of having committed grievous crimes, foremost of which are robbery, fraud, and murder.'

9

The worst of it was the silence.

The hunger was bad, and the worry and fear. The dark too, but the long and endless silence made all those things feel ten times worse than they otherwise would have.

Their money had been taken from them, and then they'd been thrown into a room at the back of the house, on the ground floor. They assumed it had been a store room of some kind, but it could not have been better designed as a prison. The stone walls were solid, cold and damp, so thick that sound would not escape. There were no windows save a slot at the top of the wall by the low ceiling, but even this was recessed deep into the thickness of the wall. It was like a small tunnel, longer than an arm, no wider than a hand. It shed sparse light and there was no thought of getting through it at all.

Their hands had been trussed behind them, and they'd been thrown into different corners, but they'd struggled to crawl over to each other, and had found a way of sitting back to back that took some of the strain off their aching arms and legs.

As they sat like this, Marko suddenly felt Sorrel's fingers touching his, and he made to move them away, but then felt her reach again and hold his fingers tight.

'Please,' he heard her whisper, and he was only too happy to do so. He held her fingers in his own, as firmly as he could manage. It was their only comfort.

They talked for a while, but it was hard. Neither of them had the strength, the will to find much hope, and could only dread what might come.

'We'll appeal to whatever court they take us to,' Marko said, with little conviction. 'They have to know that we've done nothing wrong.'

Sorrel didn't answer, and Marko remembered what she'd said about Venetian justice. Worse than that, the man they'd crossed had turned out to be one of the Three. Their chances of success looked very, very slight.

'What did he mean?' Marko asked. 'What he said about mouths?'

'Oh, that,' Sorrel said, sighing. 'Yes. The Mouths. We have a system here, for anyone who wants to make an accusation against any other person. All across the city are stone carvings, mostly lions' heads, but other faces too, of men and animals. The mouths are open, and behind is a letter box. You write down your accusation and

133

post the letter. All the letters are read by the Council of Three, and they will then decide what to do.' She stopped.

Yes, Marko had seen one of these mouths on their journey across the city the day before. He had never guessed their purpose—they'd seemed nothing more than ornaments. Sorrel explained how, in order to try and to prevent people from making false accusations, the punishment for doing so was very severe.

'If you make a false accusation, and are discovered, then you're punished as if you had committed the crime you spoke of. If you accuse someone of fraud, you're tried as a fraud. If you speak of murder, you'll be tried as a murderer.'

'And someone has accused your father through the Mouths.'

'One guess who that is,' Sorrel said.

'Venetia.'

He hesitated to ask his next question, but he had to know.

'And then?'

'Then, we will be tried by the Three. We'll be put in the cells in the Doge's palace. Maybe in the Piombi, in the attics, but more likely in the Pozzi in the basement. The Piombi are for prisoners of high status, rich men, politicians. That kind of thing. And then? Who knows?'

As they sat in the deepening silence, the light dwindled, and they knew that night was coming on again. They tried to move nearer a wall where some old sacking lay on the floor, so that perhaps they could sleep for a while. But sleep would not come, and as the darkness grew in their little prison, Sorrel felt an awful new fear creep into her.

She thought about her father, her mad father. She knew Francesco would be looking after him as well as he could, but that ultimately there was nothing he could do, if . . . if the worst were to come. Why only Marko's father Alessandro had been able to help Simono was a mystery to her, but she prayed they found him soon. Without him, her father would continue the long slide into sleeplessness, a nightmare journey that would end with a hideous death. And already she missed him, longed to see him smiling down at her again, to have him hold her hands and dance. What if he were to go for ever?

*   *   *

Sleep.

*   *   *

As the night wore on, Sorrel felt Marko's body slump against hers, and knew he was sleeping, and yet, as long as she waited, she knew that sleep was not going to come for her tonight.

She felt exhausted, but somehow with every passing minute she felt sleep was getting farther from her. Her fear grew worse still, her heart began to thump, and her mind raced.

What if . . . ?

It had happened to her father. It had happened to many people who had lived in the Ca' Bellini. What if it was happening to her?

The death of no sleep.

She began to panic and struggled with the bonds round her wrists. She whimpered to herself and

135

could bear it no longer.

'Marko! Please. Marko. Please wake up.'

Marko grunted and struggled, moaning at the stiffness in his arms and shoulders.

'Marko! Please. Oh, God.'

'What is it, Sorrel?' Marko opened his eyes in the darkness. He could see almost nothing. He felt disorientated, his senses dulled by tiredness and pain. 'What's wrong?'

'Marko! Oh God. I think it's happening to me.'

'What? What's wrong?'

He twisted, managing to shuffle round so that he was facing her, even though he could barely see her. He could sense that she was panicking, desperately frightened.

'What is it? Tell me what's wrong.'

'I think it's happening to me. I can't sleep, Marko. I can't sleep. I think it might be starting to happen to me, too.'

'No,' Marko said. 'No, you don't know that.'

'But I can't sleep! I'm so tired, but I can't. I just can't. What if it's happening to me, too?'

She began to cry, gently at first, but once she'd started, the tears seemed to take hold of her, and her cries grew worse. He felt a surge of pity for this poor strange girl, with a life so young, and yet so troubled.

Marko thought frantically. What would his father do? He tried to keep calm, though the urge to panic himself was strong. What would his father do? He thought hard and remembered a time when a local woman's child had died. She'd been hysterical from the shock. His father had given her medicine. And brandy. He had neither, but his father had spoken to the woman too. He'd talked calmly, but what had he said? Marko remembered very clearly that he hadn't tried to tell her anything she didn't want to hear, he hadn't tried to tell her everything would be all right, he'd simply spoken to her calmly until that calm had rubbed off on the poor woman.

'Sorrel,' he said, trying to think what to say. 'Sorrel. I'm here. I'm going to be here. For you. I don't think you're ill. I think you're very worried. Your body is exhausted, but your mind won't let you sleep, because you're too worried. It's only natural. It's a terrible thing that's happening to your father. To you.'

He would have liked to have added, 'to me', but bit his lip. He had to concentrate on Sorrel.

'I'm here. Whatever happens to us, I won't leave you alone. I promise. I promise.'

So he kept on talking, and gradually Sorrel grew less agitated. He leaned right in to her, and though he couldn't touch her with his hands tied, he brushed her cheek with his and spoke quietly and gently until her tears had stopped altogether.

Suddenly, Marko was aware of a small whimpering sound, and at first thought it was coming from Sorrel, but quickly he realised that the noise was coming from behind him. He turned, and saw the faint slot of grey in the blackness of the room that showed where the window recess was.

The whimpering was coming from outside, and something told Marko what was making the sound. Dog. Somehow, the little black hound had heard, or smelled, or sensed where they were, and was waiting outside.

'Dog?' Marko called softly, and the whimpering

grew louder. He knew he was right. 'Dog! It's all right. We're here. Sorrel. It's Dog. He's outside.'

He didn't know why it mattered or helped, but it was a small crumb of comfort to Marko.

Dog began to whimper louder, and Marko was wondering what to say to keep him quiet, when all of a sudden the noise stopped. Did he imagine it, or had the pale grey slot just darkened completely? He turned his eyes sideways, using the more sensitive vision to be found there in the dark, something else his father had taught him.

It was hard to tell, but maybe there was someone else out there with Dog, someone blocking the pathetic grey light that filtered into their cell.

For the next five minutes, there was total silence, a silence so profound that though they strained their ears, all they could hear was the pounding of Sorrel's heart.

'What's happening?' Sorrel whispered. She sensed, as Marko had, that something had changed. Not outside, but in the house.

'I don't . . .'

Marko was cut off as the door swung suddenly open. The light coming from behind was weak, but still enough to blind them.

All Marko could see as he blinked and squinted was a figure framed in the doorway.

10

'Well,' said a voice. 'Are you staying in here? Oh. I see. Your hands.'

The figure swept around and about them like a bat flitting through the evening air, and with two sharp tugs the ropes fell from their wrists.

'I think now it is time,' said the voice, and Marko began to recognise it. There was something familiar about the strange intonation, the order of the words.

Marko struggled to his feet. Sorrel stumbled as the numbness in her legs took hold, but the tall figure lifted her up in his arms as easily as if she was made of straw.

'Come then,' he said, and now Marko had it. It was the man from the Leon Bianco, the old man who'd plucked him from the floor when they'd collided, the old drunkard who started the fight raving some silly nonsense about vampires.

He didn't care, it could have been the devil himself in the room, as long as he was going to get them out, and that seemed to be exactly what the old man had in mind. He stooped under the low doorway with Sorrel in his arms, and Marko hurried.

The main body of the house was not in darkness, torches burned from the high walls, and suddenly, in the most awful fashion, Marko had the answer to the question uppermost in his mind. How on earth had the old man simply walked into the house?

Here was the answer. They were back in the large hallway that led to the street. The old man had not messed around. Beppe, the doorman, lay sprawled on the floor, a vast cut opening his belly from side to side. Sorrel shrieked and the old man reached up from under her with his left hand and clamped it over her mouth.

139

'Ssssh,' he hissed. 'There may be others to come.'

They reached the door, which stood ajar, but as they went, Marko turned to see three more bodies in the large reception room where they'd met Bruno. At least three, each of them still and bloody.

Terror grabbed Marko by the throat, and began to squeeze tight. They were through the door and out in the street, and there, Dog was waiting for them. He leaped up at the sight of Marko, who stopped to ruffle his ears, but the man was striding quickly away down a narrow calle, towards the canal, and Marko followed hurriedly. They were free, but my God, he thought, was this the devil who'd come to free them? He tried to keep up, but the man moved fast, even with Sorrel in his arms.

He turned to Marko briefly.

'Hurry. We must go now,' his voice urgent, and strong.

How old was he?

Marko dimly wondered how a man who looked at least seventy could be so powerful, and move so fast. They climbed down into a small burchiello that was moored to the jetty. The boat bobbed and heaved in the sucking black water, torchlight flickered all around them, sparkling like jewels on the endlessly moving surface of the canal, and then they were gone, as the man pushed them out into the stream and away from number 5696, Canareggio.

They were back on the Grand Canal, at night, just as they had been the evening Marko had arrived, only a couple of days before. So much had changed in that short time, so much had happened, that it seemed to Marko a lifetime had passed.

It was well into late evening, yet there was life on the canal, and in the palazzo overlooking it. Marko watched idly for a while, but Sorrel seemed to be in shock. She sat mute in the covered section in the middle of the boat. Marko sat next to her, but faced the back of the boat, where the old man skulled the single oar through the water, like a natural born gondolier. Only now did Marko see the point of a long scabbard poking from the man's robes. The same weapon which had saved them on San Michele, he knew.

Dog lay in his usual place, keeping Marko's toes warm. Marko wondered which question to ask first.

Who are you?

What are you doing here?

Why did you help us?

But he said nothing, and instead put an arm around Sorrel, who turned and smiled.

'Are we free?'

Marko nodded.

'But what about him?' she whispered. 'Dear God! Those bodies . . .'

She fell silent.

'Here!' the man called to them. 'I put you down here. You will be safe now.'

He began to pull into the far bank of the Canal, and Marko realised with a mixture of relief and fear that he was going to let them go. The relief he could understand. The man killed without compunction. He was obviously some sort of madman, a lunatic. That would explain his extraordinary strength. His father had told him of such things, and now Marko had seen it for himself, but the fear? Why fear? Because there was something about the man that was so . . . comforting. That was the word. Marko realised he felt safe being near him. He'd just marched into a strange house guarded by some very ruthless men, swept them aside, and pulled Marko and Sorrel to safety.

'Wait!' he said. 'It was you. On San Michele. You saved us there, too, didn't you?'

At first the old man appeared not to hear Marko, intent as he was on putting into a quiet little landing stage, quite deserted, but then he looked at Marko.

'You were there?' he said, casually. 'I thought I recognised your girl. I thought she was dead. I am pleased she is not. If you were there, then . . .'

He shrugged, as if to say, what of it?

'I was in another room. But you saved us there and you saved us again tonight.'

'You are not happy?'

'No, no, it's just . . .'

'You killed those people,' Sorrel said, finding her voice. 'You killed all those people.'

'Yes', the old man nodded. 'Yes, I did.'

'You can't do that. No matter who they are. You cannot just kill people so easily.'

There was a long and awful silence, which

142

seemed to be the old man's way of saying, *But I can.*

'You can go, and be safe now.'

He pointed to the bank, but Marko and Sorrel didn't move.

'Wait,' Marko said. 'You have helped us twice, but there's more going on here. We're in trouble. My father is missing somewhere in the city, we have to find him. Sorrel's father is ill and only my father can help. We both need him.'

'What of it?'

He reached with one hand now to grasp a post that jutted from the water by the landing stage, and kept the heavy craft moored alongside the jetty. There was something truly unsettling about it.

'It can't be chance that you've turned up twice just when we needed your help. It's like a miracle, like something supernatural.'

Marko waited for an answer. He didn't get one, but the old man's air of disinterest had gone.

'Why did you kill those men? Why are you helping us?' Marko threw his hands in the air. 'Who *are* you?'

The old man let go of the post he'd been holding and let the burchiello drift into the canal again.

'Yes,' he said thoughtfully, as if changing his mind. 'You are right. I see it all now. I see it all.'

He swished the oar into the water once again, and the boat nosed south.

'I know a safer place,' he said. 'Rest now. Be still, and then we will talk. Sometimes life is like this, that these things happen, and they happen for a reason. It may be that you can help me, and that

143

I can help you.'

So they went, and as they did so, Marko had the strangest feeling that neither his relief nor his fear had vanished, but that they had simply switched places with each other.

12

From high above Venice a pair of black eyes watched the city, seeing her plans unfold. She saw her disciples everywhere, in all the sestieres, and a deep and true knowledge of what she was going to do welled up inside her shrunken white chest.

She smiled in satisfaction.

From her vantage point, nearly touching the stars, her keen vision spotted one of her newest recruits staggering like a drunkard into the gambling house, just as she'd whispered in his ear two nights ago in the forsaken little calle where she'd found him. He'd responded easily to her suggestions, and now she saw three others greet him, and take him upstairs. They pulled off the man's shirt and sat him in a chair, pushing his head down onto a table on which were placed a bowl of blue black ink and various dirty-looking needles.

One of the men wiped a filthy cloth across the newcomer's neck, in a vain attempt to clean it, and then set to, etching out the first letter. A small, neat 'V'.

The man twitched against the pain and the tattooist jolted away, in frustration. He shouted something to the other two who grabbed their victim's arms and shoulders, then got to work again.

Yes, it hurt. But they'd all had it done, and lived. This one would be no different.

A Fairy Tale

Then, one day in the autumn, the peasant girl who had been a princess, had a baby, a beautiful baby boy, and the couple were so happy that the girl almost forgot where she had come from and who she really was.

Winter came early that year, and stayed for a long time, and things grew hard for everyone. The young couple struggled to keep themselves warm, and they struggled to feed themselves, and their baby. The young man tried to sell as much wood as he could cut, but everyone was starving, and no one had food to spare. Door after door was closed against them, until one day, the one-time princess had no choice but to swallow her pride, knock on the great doors of the castle, and ask her father for help. The King had changed, and had become a bitter and vicious ruler. All his people were starving in the grip of the terrible winter, and he either would not, or could not help them.

'Who?' he asked, when they told him his daughter was at the gates. 'Who? I have but two daughters, now queens, and they are far from here in warmer kingdoms, with their good husbands. Whoever the girl is, send her away! She is no queen!'

With that, the girl stumbled away in the snow, back towards her hovel, and her husband and child.

'Oh God! Is there no one to help us?' she wailed, and when no answer came, she cried out again. 'Not even God will help me. The devil would be kinder!'

With that, she collapsed in the snow.

*   *   *

A little time later, she felt a hand at her elbow, and found herself looking into the face of a wizened old man of the woods, helping her to her feet. She was startled, and shrank away from him, for there was something about him that she did not like, but he merely smiled back.

'My dear,' he said. 'I heard you call out. I think you are in a predicament, and I think I may be able to help. I can grant you one wish, and you have my word that whatever you wish for will come true.'

'Is it true?' asked the girl, too frightened to think.

'It is true,' said the old man, nodding. 'Just one wish.'

'Then,' said the girl, 'I wish that my baby and my husband will never go hungry again!'

The man smiled.

'But that,' he said, 'is so easy. Nevertheless, it is done! Go home now, and be warm.'

He walked away into the snow, and the girl was so excited that she never even saw that where the man had walked, he left behind not foot prints, but hoof prints.

She ran the rest of the way home, and burst in through the door to tell her husband the incredible promise she had been given, and she saw that her wish had been granted, for there lay her husband on the floor, and her baby in the cot, with not a breath of life between them.

They would never go hungry again.

FOUR

'So, tell me. What do you know of the world?

It seemed a strange sort of question, but then this was turning out to be a very strange night.

The old man had rowed them through the narrowest canals in the heart of the city, heading east, and even Sorrel had lost her sense of direction. Somehow though, their dreadful saviour seemed to know exactly where he was going. At last they emerged in more open water, and Sorrel recognised the walls of the Arsenale ahead.

Even though it was the middle of the night the sounds of work drifted over the high protective walls of the military harbour of the city. Inside, carpenters and shipwrights were still working on the Bucintoro for the Doge's procession. Each dreaming of the rewards if they finished in time, and dreading the punishments if they did not.

The boat turned again, and then the old man moored up, leading the way under a low archway, down a stinking alley, and into the abandoned log store in which they now sat.

To their immense discomfort, it appeared that he had been living in this slum for some time. Even Dog circled more than usual, trying to find somewhere clean to rest his belly.

Nevertheless, that was where they now sitting, and while Marko and Sorrel chewed on some dried ham he'd given them, the old man made a small fire round which they warmed themselves, though choking on the smoke, with no chimney. Dog lay on the ground, eyeing the ham enviously. The old man laughed and found a piece for him, too.

'Yes,' he said, talking to Dog. 'You deserve something. You saved your master tonight, did you not? Showed me where they were.'

'Were you looking for us?' Marko said with wonder. 'Were you following us?'

'Not you.'

'Then who?'

'What do you know of the world?' he said. 'What have you seen?'

Marko refused to answer, he had plenty of questions of his own.

'Why did you change your mind? About leaving us just now? You know something, don't you? What do you know? What have you done? Tell us your name, at least.'

The old man swung his gaze from Marko to the fire, to Sorrel and back to the fire.

'I am called Peter,' he said eventually, as though it had been a struggle. 'I am called Peter, but no one has called me anything for a long time. It is not important. Not anymore. And you.'

He turned to Sorrel.

'You are the daughter of Simono Bellini. You are the English girl, but I forget your name.'

'Sorrel. And I'm half Venetian,' she said. Marko smiled at her, she seemed at last to be feeling herself again.

'Yes, yes, we are all mongrels here. Do not be ashamed.'

'Mongrels!' Sorrel spluttered. 'Who do you . . .'

'We are all mongrels. You are half-English, half Venetian. I am a mongrel. My father was city born, my mother was a gypsy. And you?'

He looked at Marko.

152

'You. You are like me too. Your father is Venetian, but your skin tells me your mother is from somewhere to the east of here. Yes.'

'You know my father?' Marko exclaimed, but Peter ignored him.

'And our friend on the floor. He is the last of us four mongrels.'

Marko grew angry.

'Tell me what you know about my father. For God's sake!'

'Yes. I know your father,' Peter said. 'I know both your fathers, though they do not know me. And I only realised I know who you are in the boat. Something you said about San Michele. Then I recognised this pretty girl!

'My poor children, I must tell you things that are not very good. But your fathers are alive, yes, both of them. The doctor Alessandro, is in prison. In the Doge's palace. He has been accused of witchcraft, of heresy, and will be tried very soon. This is difficult, because I want to talk to him very much.'

Marko's spirits leaped at the news of his father. He had forced himself to believe that he was still alive, but until now, he had not really known. The relief made him want to laugh and cry.

Peter was not finished.

'Yes, this is very difficult. To free him from there I think is impossible, even for me. And I need to talk to him. He can help me, I think, just as he was helping Simono.'

At her father's name, Sorrel began to tremble. Somehow she could not keep her eyes from straying to the long scabbard inside which she knew was the terrible weapon which had taken the men's lives away.

'Please,' she said quietly. 'What do you know about my father? Do you know what's wrong with him?'

Peter shook his head.

'I do not. Though I think I know what has broken his mind.'

This statement seemed to make Sorrel angry, but Marko spoke before she could.

'What? Who?'

Peter turned to Marko.

'You are a clever boy. I think you have listened to your father. He has taught you how to think. It was something that took me many more years to learn. I only used to know how to feel, and that is something quite different. And that is why I ask of you, what do you know of the world? Of hidden things?'

Sorrel nodded.

'But who?' she asked. 'Do you mean the Council of Ten? The Three? The Inquisitors?'

'No. It is much more serious than that.'

'How can it be worse than that?'

Peter raised a hand as if making an oath.

'This is why I say to you; what do you know of life? What have you seen? What do you believe? Because you will need to think again about these things. Do you understand?'

Marko shook his head. It was all too much to take in, let alone understand.

Sorrel whispered quietly, 'I don't understand anything.'

'Then it would be best to tell you a story. It is not a happy story, but it may help you to understand. It will explain things to you, so that

154

you can see that everything is connected, everything.'

2

'I am not from Venice,' Peter said, as if it were not obvious. 'I am from a long way away, from a land beyond the forests. Closer to where your mother is from, I think, Marko. I grew up there with my father. My mother, I never knew. My father and I moved about. We did all sorts of things, but most of the time we worked as woodcutters in the deep forests, moving from place to place, until one day we came to a small village.

And there I knew that I had known nothing of the world, that I had only seen a small fraction of its joys, and yes, its horrors too. Because there, I fell in love, and there I discovered the true nature of the evil in the world.

'I fell in love with a wonderful girl, a gypsy.' He smiled now, and his eyes twinkled with some distant fondness. 'I know her name, better than I know mine. Sophia.'

He breathed her name, a sigh, and for a while, said nothing more. Then he snapped himself from his thoughts.

'She taught me much. She helped me to understand my father, but in the end, no one could save him. He died trying to save us all. From them.'

His voice had dropped to a whisper, and Marko's followed suit.

'Who?'

155

'Those who live after death. Those people who are hostages to her great evil, those who come back to take others with them. You would call them, I think, vampyri.'

'Vampires!' Sorrel shouted. 'That's ridiculous.'

Peter said nothing, but slammed one hand into the other in a gesture of anger.

'No, please,' cried Marko. 'Don't listen to her. Please tell us. Please?'

'Marko, don't tell me you believe this. Vampires! What would your father say about thinking something like that? Come on. Let's stop wasting time.'

She began to make for the low door, when Peter swung back towards them.

'Yes!' he roared. 'What would your father say? Now that he is locked in the Piombi? Or your father? Now that he is out of his mind!'

Marko turned to Sorrel.

'Listen to me. Listen. I saw something. Twice. On those men, the ones . . .'

He looked nervously up at Peter.

'The ones I killed?'

Marko nodded.

'What?' asked Sorrel.

'There were marks, on the backs of their necks. All of them. It was a tattoo. There was a skull, and above it, the word vampyri . . .'

'That doesn't mean they're really vampires,' Sorrel said. 'There are all sorts of secret societies in Venice, they often brand themselves with some mark or other. What you saw was probably just that. Not real vampires.'

'You are both right,' Peter said before Marko could answer. 'Yes, Sorrel, there are really such creatures as vampires, but no, Marko, I don't think these men with tattoos are such things. I would know, trust me, I would know. I think they are playing a deadly game of vampires, and yet, there is someone here who is controlling them, someone I have been hunting all my life, ever since that village in the forest. She is an ancient being now, but her intent is terrible, she will never rest. She goes by various names, but I call her by the one I first heard. The Shadow Queen. I have followed her for years, ages it seems to me, and I have found her at last.

'She is here, in Venice.'

3

The fire began to fade as they spoke, and by the time it had died completely, Marko believed every word that Peter told them. There was something in his voice, something about his manner, that compelled him to believe, and so believe he did.

He told them of the years of travelling, fighting the creatures he called hostages.

'Because, you see, it is not their fault that they are what they are. They are taken prisoner, their very souls become hostage to the thing that makes them into these monsters. Over time they have changed, they have become more sophisticated creatures, they have changed their habits, become harder to see, harder to kill, and yet, I have changed too. For when I started, I was only full of horror and hate for these things, but as the years passed I began to understand the old name for

157

them, "hostages", and I came even to pity them. Though that is not to say that I had to stop what I was doing. I could no more stop killing them, than the farmer who kills the sheep with the broken back. It is pity that makes us do so.

'And with every one I set free, there is one fewer to create more. My life has been very long, and I have been very successful. I believe there are very few of them left now, very few indeed. I think I have taken something from the Shadow Queen, over the years, that her powers are growing weaker.'

Sorrel gazed at the old man.

'How long have you been doing this?' she asked gently.

'Oh,' said Peter, and his old face cracked into a smile. 'Oh, since I was his age.'

He waved a hand at Marko.

'And when was that?'

'When? The year you mean?'

Sorrel nodded.

'I think I remember that in that following winter we went to a place called Reval. It was sixteen hundred and twenty five.'

Sorrel sat up.

'No,' she said, but kindly. 'You must be mistaken. That would make you well over a hundred years old.'

Peter stood up from the fire.

'No,' he said simply, and picked up the scabbard and the sword within it. 'I know the year, because I had the man put Sophia's name on one side, and the date on the other. That was the year we were married.'

He tipped the end of the scabbard towards

Sorrel, as if he was suggesting she pulled the sword from the sheath, but instead he jabbed an old finger towards the date. There it was, embossed in the leather.

1625.

Peter sat down again, and stroked Dog's head, who snuffled contentedly.

Sorrel looked at Marko, her eyes wide with wonder and fear at this strange old man who had saved their skins twice.

Marko opened his mouth, shut it again, and shook his head, thinking just the same as Sorrel. He had to be mad, or deluded, which was the same thing, and yet . . . There was something about him which made them doubt their doubt.

Peter was still, and the fire went out.

4

The old man seemed to be asleep; his head rested on some sacking, his eyes closed.

Marko and Sorrel whispered to each other in the darkness. Dog snored and whimpered alternately. Occasionally his paws flicked and Marko hoped he was dreaming of rabbit chases in sunny meadows, rather than being hunted by foul men through the streets of Venice.

'What should we do?' Sorrel asked.

'God, Sorrel. I don't know. I can't think straight. I'm so tired.'

'I know,' she said. 'But listen, do you think we can trust him?'

'Peter?' Marko lowered his voice even further.

'That depends on what you mean. He could have killed us twice over, and instead he saved us twice over. He didn't have to do that.'

'I know, but he did it as if we were of no importance to him. As if we don't matter.'

'I don't think we do,' Marko said, 'to him. But he's at least a good enough man to save us, since he could. I think we're safe with him. The question is rather . . .'

'. . . whether he's going to help us.' Sorrel finished Marko's sentence, and added, 'And we don't have much time. The procession is tomorrow afternoon; if we don't make peace with Venetia somehow by then . . .'

'Venetia's the least of our problems, I keep telling you.'

'I know. I know.'

'But he said he wants my father's help. At least he's alive.'

'And we know where he is, but . . .'

'What?' Marko asked.

'I'm afraid he's right. No one escapes from the Piombi. They might let you go, once enough years have passed, but Marko, you should know there's usually only one way people leave that place.'

She didn't need to explain what she meant, and Marko's head fell.

'Maybe he *can* help us,' Sorrel said quickly. 'Maybe . . .'

'Maybe,' Marko said, 'he's just an old madman, a murderous old lunatic, and we're just lucky he seems not to feel about us the way he feels about everyone else he meets.'

'I thought you believed what he was saying?'

'I don't know,' Marko said. 'But I tell you this,

160

I'm not sitting here any longer. We're going.'

He sat up, and began to stoop towards the door.

'Where?'

'Yes. Where?'

They turned and saw Peter sitting upright, wide awake.

'Where are you going? To the Piombi? And what would you do there? Against the guards of the Ducal palace? But yes, it is time to go, and if you will trust an old lunatic, then you will come with me.'

After an awkward moment of silence in which Marko and Sorrel realised they'd been overheard, Sorrel found her voice.

'Wherc? Where are we going?'

'To Giudecca,' Peter said, and jabbed a finger at Sorrel. 'To your house.'

5

The three, Peter, Marko and Sorrel, and the ever present shadow of Dog, crossed the water to the tip of Giudecca. Away to their right, torchlight on the waterfront lit the Doge's palace with a luminous red glow. Marko's heart wrenched, burned with it, burned with the knowledge that just across the water, in the attic cells of that very building, his father lay mouldering in some windowless cell.

Every stroke took them farther away. Peter stood at the back of the burchiello, and this time, on the open water, Sorrel helped from the front with another oar. Marko had tried at first, but couldn't manage the strange standing rowing position that it demanded. Sorrel, to his surprise, was much stronger than she looked.

'Francesco taught me,' she explained. 'Though Father doesn't like me doing it.'

Dog stood on the prow of the boat, sniffing the air, and soon the island approached through the night, which was clear and free from mist for once.

Sorrel stared forwards as she tried to pick out the Ca' Bellini. As they made the headland they ought to be able to see it, taller as it was than most other houses on Giudecca.

At the back of the boat, out of earshot of Sorrel, Marko asked Peter, 'Why are we going here?'

'I have been slow to think tonight, Marko,' the old man said. 'I have been as slow as my years are long. I have been foolish. I think Bruno or his men will come for her father.'

'Bruno? Didn't . . . ? I mean, didn't you . . . ?'

'No, I did not kill him. He was not in the house when I came for you. Rest assured, I would kill him if he was there. He is the cause of much of this I think. He is deep in all this.'

'How?'

'I do not know that. I have been watching, for many months. I have moved from here to here in the city, watching, listening. I knew that something was spreading through the city like the plagues of old. And all the time, the paths that I followed led me back to this man. Nicolo Bruno. Then I discovered that he is a powerful man, and I began to fear. This is often the way, evil finds its root in the great and powerful; those who cannot be accused, who cannot be deposed so easily. It is another layer of protection for them, you

162

understand?'

'But you think his men will come for Simono. Why? He's just a crazy old man.'

'Perhaps. I was foolish. I have not seen the patterns here. There are still some patterns I do not understand, but I fear for Simono now. His daughter is clever, but she is not with him. We ought to be there. He has only the servants to defend him should they come.'

'No,' said Marko, shaking his head. 'They all left. There's only one, Francesco.'

Peter cursed in a language he didn't understand.

'Then we have been even more foolish. We must hurry. They will come tonight if they have not come already.'

At the front of the boat, Sorrel had discovered the source of her fear.

'Look!' she cried back to them. 'There are no lights. There's the house, but there are no lights.'

Marko tried to reassure her.

'It's the middle of the night, they may be sleeping.'

As soon as the words were out of his mouth, he realised what he'd said.

'My father will not be sleeping,' Sorrel said, and Marko held up a hand to apologise.

As they turned into the canal which led to the house, their worst fears were realised. The front door flapped open in the wind that swung in from the south lagoon.

'No!' Sorrel cried.

They put in, but even before the boat had touched the embankment, Sorrel sprang from the prow. Dog sensed the excitement and leaped after her, and the pair were inside the doors of the

163

darkened house before Peter had tied the boat.

'No!' he shouted. 'It may not be safe. There may be . . .'

Marko ran after Sorrel, and felt the creeping dread again as he watched a man of supposedly a hundred years overtake him in two long strides. As he went, Peter pulled the sword from its scabbard in a single fluid motion, brandishing it behind and above him as if ready to swing it down without warning. The sword seemed to give a sighing sound as it emerged into the night, a swish, that almost seemed alive to Marko. It was as if the sword was singing to itself. Pushing this ludicrous notion from his mind, he trailed into the hall and saw Peter bounding up the stairs to the first floor.

He gave chase, and caught up with Dog, as they hunted from room to room.

Suddenly there was a scream from Sorrel.

'Here!'

It was impossible to tell where the call had come from, but he saw Peter hurrying along the second floor landing, towards Simono's bedroom.

He rushed up, and burst into the room to find Sorrel crouched over a figure, Peter striding round, his sword flashing in the darkness, and Dog skittering here and there, unsure of what to do.

Marko knelt by Sorrel who crouched over Francesco.

He was alive, but seemed badly shaken, and a little blood stained the faded carpets beneath him.

Sorrel lifted Francesco's head and felt her hand dampen. She pulled it away.

'What?' she asked frantically. 'What happened? Are you all right?'

Francesco nodded gently.

'Have they taken Father?' she cried.

The mute nodded, closing his eyes to show pain.

'Who? Where?'

'Wait, Sorrel,' Marko said. 'One question at a time.'

He looked at Peter.

'Can you find some water?' he asked, but the old man seemed to have entered some kind of trance, some fighting state, as he prowled around the room. Marko cursed and turned to Francesco.

'Have they taken Simono?'

The mute nodded.

'Where?'

Francesco shook his head. He didn't know.

'Who? Did you recognise them?'

Again he shook his head.

'Was there a fat man? I mean, a really fat man?'

Once more, the shake of his head.

'He wouldn't come himself.'

Peter stared down at the scene on the floor. He spoke in portentous tones, his blood still swimming with the prospect of violence.

'He would not come himself. She has an army of men to do these things, and he is just one part of that army.'

'Did they say anything?' Sorrel asked Francesco, but again he shook his head. 'Are you all right? Are you hurt?'

Francesco managed to sit up, and put a hand to his neck.

'Here, let me see,' Sorrel said, but Francesco pushed her away, and managed to lift himself onto his master's bed, then he pointed, and thrust his finger, jabbing it, until they understood.

'He means we should go. We should go and find

165

Simono.'

Sorrel grabbed Francesco's hand and kissed it.

'We will. We will. But what about you?'

Francesco waved her away, began pointing again. He indicated the bed.

'He'll be all right,' Marko said. 'I'll find him some water.'

'But where? Where are we going to look for him?'

The question fell into the silence of the room, and no one answered it, at least, not at first, then Peter stepped away from the bed and looked out at the city.

'They are massing. I know her. She is massing her armies, but for that they will need space, somewhere they cannot be seen, while they prepare themselves. I believe they need Simono, that his illness and his genius are all connected to this. And that is where they have taken him.'

'But where?' cried Marko. 'He could be anywhere, the city is so large.'

'No, not the city, I think. It is too crowded, too busy. They need somewhere secluded.'

'Like the islands? Sorrel said.

'Yes, perhaps,' said Peter.

'But there are so many of them,' Sorrel cried. 'They could be anywhere.'

'No.'

Peter and Sorrel turned to Marko, who stood at another window, that looked south across the lagoon.

'No. Not anywhere. I know where they are.'

They followed his gaze, and there, near the horizon, they saw what Marko had seen, what he'd seen on his first night in Venice. Bonfires on a

166

distant island.

'Tell me, Sorrel,' he said. 'What is that place? Does anyone live there?'

'My God,' she whispered. 'You're right. That's Lazaretto. No one lives there. Not any more. No one even goes there, not even fishermen.'

'Why not?'

'Because it's the old plague island. Everyone shuns it now, but during the plagues it was where the sick were sent. It has awful stories, terrible memories. If you became ill with the plague you were sent there. If you were still alive after thirty days, they let you come back. Very few ever did. Since then it's just been empty. No one goes there.'

'No?' Marko said. 'Well, there's someone there now.'

Peter stooped to look out of the window more easily, and clapped a hand on Marko's shoulder.

'Yes, you are a clever one,' he said. 'Yes.'

And was it their imagination, or even at this great distance, staring at the flickering light of those remote fires, was it possible to see figures leaping and dancing in front of the flames?

They readied themselves to go.

They left Francesco in Simono's bed. He kept pointing, urging them to hurry.

They found some blankets and coats. Sorrel went to her room, and changed into one of her own dresses.

'That's more like it,' she said.

'Yes,' said Marko. 'Well, it is black.'

Peter went to the kitchen and returned with two long knives for Sorrel and Marko, putting them into their hands as carefully as if they were precious and delicate jewellery.

167

Dog ran around, and then sensing they were ready to go, stood stock still.

'So,' Peter said. 'She is massing her armies, and in reply, we have ours. Us three.'

Dog gave a single short bark, and Marko laughed.

'I think that means four,' he said.

* * *

They left, and as the burchiello slipped away from the bank, a face watched from the first floor window. Francesco had got out of bed the moment he heard the front door close, and now stood far enough back not to be seen.

He rubbed the back of his neck. Yes, there was a little blood, but it was not so bad really. The funny thing was that he could still smell the ink they'd used. That blue-black ink. He wondered if they got it from squids.

He made his way downstairs.

6

'Hurry!' Peter whispered through the darkness. As they passed under the balcony of the beautiful Venetia's house Sorrel cursed silently, and for a moment thought she heard the strains of singing floating down to them, but she knew she had to be imagining it; it was the small hours of the night now, the dog watch.

She spat into the water, and made a promise to herself. If they found Simono, and rescued

Alessandro, she would stop Venetia from hurting her family again. No matter what it took.

Sorrel rowed until her arms burned and her shoulders with them, and then she collapsed into the centre of the boat. Marko tried the rowing motion again, and having watched Sorrel made a better go of it, but in truth, their great speed came from Peter, who silently worked at the stern of the boat, repeating the forward and back snake of his arms again and again, with no sign even of breathlessness. Occasionally he flicked his arms a couple of times to the side to correct their steering, but otherwise he powered them as though the devil was behind them, and the black water of the lagoon shushed past on either side like rapids in a fast-flowing river.

Sorrel gazed up at Peter, and moved cautiously down the length of the boat to the covered section towards the stern.

'Who are you?' she said quietly. She did not mean that Peter should hear, or that he should answer, but it seemed his hearing was as powerful as his arms.

'You don't mean that, do you?' he said. His voice sailed easily to her against the slight breeze from their movement forwards. Marko caught his words, and half turned, trying to hear and row at the same time. 'You don't mean that. What you mean, is *what* am I? Yes?'

Sorrel nodded.

'I'm sorry. I don't mean to be rude, but you are . . . impossible. The things you do. I have worked it out. You must be about a hundred and twenty five years old. No one lives that long, and even a thirty-year-old man could not do the things you can do.'

169

She stopped, and having been asked no question, Peter did not answer. Sorrel swallowed hard.

'Are you,' she said, 'the devil?'

Peter laughed, a thick rasping croak.

'Why not an angel? No? I could be either I suppose, but you choose the bad one. No, I am only a man. It is not me that does these things, or perhaps I should say, I was not born this way. I was a woodcutter's son, as I told you, but . . . it is the sword. The sword has made me this way.'

'What do you mean?'

Peter didn't slow his rowing in the slightest degree, nor did he move his eyes from the firelight dancing ahead of them.

'I think it is the sword that has changed me. I noticed only after a few years. It is very subtle. Every time I used the sword to release the soul of a hostage, I felt something. At first I thought it was the thrill of it, and I felt guilty for this, so I didn't speak of it. I was ashamed that I felt pleasure. A pleasure, of sorts. But then, as I continued to use the sword, I looked at what it was that happened, and I realised that it was not something I was feeling in my heart, but a real, physical thing. Every soul I freed, every life I ended, seemed to give me something. I felt something enter into me, and I found I was stronger.

'At first I thought it was a wonderful thing. This sword, you see, was made in Turkey, years ago. Very many years ago. And it was made to free hostages, to stop this plague of death. It was giving me the strength to do it, and so I was delighted with the power it gave to me, to help me in my fight. But then, one day, as my wife and I travelled

170

through a high mountain pasture, we stopped to make camp for the night. The sound of cowbells drifted up to us from the meadows below, and we were suddenly very, very hungry, and eager to eat, and sleep.

'It was coming on to evening, and though it was late spring, there was still snow on the highest peaks. The sun was setting, and I remember that two larks were circling in the air, calling to each other, some way below us in the valley. It was, I think, the most beautiful moment of my whole life.

'I called to Sophia, and bid her look at the larks. "They are like us, my love," I said, laughing. "Still so much in love." And then I turned to look at Sophia, and I saw something I had not seen before. I saw lines on her face, even through her dark gypsy skin, deep lines around her eyes. "We are getting old, Sophia," I said, and then, she turned to me, and she said, "Yes, Peter. I have been getting old for some time, but no, not you . . . You are still a young man." And then she lifted one of my hands to her face, and put my other hand on my own face. "There," she said.'

Peter stopped for a moment, his mind far away, but still his arms pumped like the devil. Marko had stopped rowing altogether to listen, and his oar trailed in the water, as Peter resumed his story.

'Still I didn't believe it at first, but next time we came to a town, Sophia bought a looking-glass to prove it to me. "How long have you known?" I asked, and she said she'd been watching it for many years. "Haven't you noticed the miles we've travelled, my dear?" she asked. "The summers that have come and gone?" I shook my head. I'd been too busy fighting, too busy doing what I thought I

171

had to do, and I had not seen my wife grow old. My own face, in the mirror, was that of a young man, while Sophia told me that she had spent over forty summers with me, since we'd met.

'And then I knew that what the sword had done to me was a dreadful thing. That it is evil to me, even though it does good for others. That the sword was giving me the lives of everyone it killed, making me stronger, slowing down the rate at which I grew old. It must have done the same to my father too, at first, though then he stopped using it for years, until that final time . . . But still he may have been much older than I thought.

'So I went on fighting, and following wherever I heard word of that hideous and ancient beast, the Shadow Queen. And at last I think I have run her to ground.'

Sorrel's voice trembled, like the water of the lagoon.

'And what about Sophia, what happened to her?'

Peter finally stopped rowing, and let the boat drift for a time.

'She died,' he said simply. 'She died the following year. She was not so old, but not so young either. "The miles have worn me down," she said, and one day she went to sleep and never woke again. I made a pyre and burned her so that she would never be able to become one of my enemies, and then I took her ashes back to that mountainside, where I had first learned the truth. I scattered them from the highest spot I could find, and, do you know, I saw those two larks again, circling in the sunset. And I knew that we were still like those two love birds, even though she had gone ahead of me.

'"Ah," I said, to the mountain winds. "Is this, perhaps, death?" And I thought I heard the winds answer me. "Yes," they said. "This is death, but not for you. Not for you."'

With that, Peter grasped the oar tightly again, and the boat surged forwards.

'It won't be long now,' he said, but neither Marko nor Sorrel knew if he was talking about their arrival at Lazaretto, or something else, entirely.

7

Lazaretto, the plague island, was suddenly right before them, looming out of the darkness, bathed in a glow as if all the devils of hell were stamping their feet and making bright sparks fly from their heels.

'Silence,' Peter said. 'Be still. Lie down in the boat.'

Marko and Sorrel did as they were bid, and Marko gently stroked Dog's ears to make sure he was happy and calm.

Even Peter knelt by the stern now, in case he cast any kind of silhouette that might be seen from the shore. With one hand he flicked the oar from time to time, just enough to keep the boat moving silently across the water. He turned the nose of the burchiello, so they were moving alongside the bank of the island, a short distance out. They approached the harbour, dozens of small boats and one or two larger ones lay moored to a series of landing platforms sticking out of the black water, but Peter rowed on and left it behind, obviously seeking a more private place to make landfall.

Marko gazed at the vague shapes he could see in the darkness.

'Aren't there any houses at all?' he whispered to Sorrel.

'No, only ruins. It's been a long time since the plague. No one comes here. It's an evil place.'

It took little more to convince Marko of that. As they glided past the dark banks of Lazaretto, they caught the occasional whiff of bonfire, and the comparison to hell was even easier to make. He pictured how it must have been during the plague time. Ten thousand people on this tiny speck of an island, and all dying or dead from the Black Death. He saw it all before him; the crush of the people, the awful sights. The noise of groaning and wailing. The bark of dogs, the circling carrion birds overhead. Some going mad from the horror of it all, running and screaming like the damned, throwing themselves into the lagoon, swimming for the mainland, either to drown, or be drowned by the guards on watch.

Marko was lost in these awful images, when suddenly there was a flash of golden sparks, a shower that chased upwards into the starry sky. Someone had stirred one of the big bonfires into life and sent its seeds skittering into the air, picked out like shimmering stars among the thick plumes of black smoke that were almost invisible in the darkness.

With this tumult of fire, a loud hullabaloo rose from the island, something between a moan and a

174

cheer, and with it, although they could not yet be seen, Marko and Sorrel realised for the first time just how very many people there were at this infernal pageant.

The hair rose on the back of Marko's neck, and Dog gave a low growl.

'Yes, Dog,' Marko whispered. 'I feel it too.'

8

The shower of sparks flared again, throwing wild swirling patterns into the night sky, mixing with the thick smoke, forming a living tower that roared upwards with great and terrible fury.

Marko and Sorrel cowered in the bottom of Peter's boat, as he swished his oar purposefully through the water, propelling them without a sound a little distance off shore. Dog lifted his head from between Marko's arms, sniffing the air. He whimpered quietly, and Marko knew how he felt, because he felt the same; an all-consuming fear was spreading through his bones and his belly. He turned to look at Sorrel in the wavering light thrown from the massive bonfire and saw the same fear reflected on her face too. He watched Peter and on his face he saw nothing. Not one emotion played across the old man's features, not fear, not doubt, not excitement, not even interest. The only thing Marko could read there was a look of concentration, and he knew that Peter was entering that state they'd seen him in at the Ca' Bellini. He was preparing to act, and Marko almost felt sorry for whoever stood in his way.

175

Another loud cheer rose from the place of the fire, and Marko turned his head back to the island, as Peter started edging the boat closer inshore, looking for a place to land, unseen. The din was lifting up from beyond the ruins that lay near the banks of Lazaretto, a crumbling silhouette of brick, stone and wooden beams, behind which they would be well obscured from view. Peter suddenly made his choice and with a flick of the oar they were heading into shore.

'There's no jetty,' Peter called. 'Marko. Leap ashore and pull our nose onto the mud.'

Marko turned to argue, then saw the look on Peter's face. It told him there would be nothing to be gained by arguing and so, pulling a grim face, he crept to the prow of the burchiello and waited to time his jump ashore. Here the land didn't fall straight into the water like almost everywhere else in Venice, but was a natural shallow beach of mud, weed and gravel, and Marko wanted to avoid the worst of it if he could.

He jumped, and as he did, he heard a low chant begin to sound from the devilish party beyond the ruins. The boat glided into the mud behind him and he turned and gave it an extra tug to get it safely ashore, its nose on the land and its stern gently afloat still. Peter strode down the length of the boat and pulled Sorrel with him, leaping as far over the water as he could.

'Safely done, Marko,' he said, striding past, and without hesitation headed for the ruins nearby.

Sorrel found Marko in the darkness.

'Where's that dog?' he whispered. 'Where is he?'

'He seems nervous.'

Dog stood at the grounded prow, hesitating. He lifted one front foot then the other, dithering, sniffing the air again, the whiskers above his eyes twitching.

'Come on, Dog,' Marko whispered. Then, a little more firmly, 'Come on. You'll be safer with us.'

Dog waited a moment more, then finally leaped from the boat, landing right at Marko's feet.

'We'd better tie it up, just to make sure,' Sorrel said, pulling the painter from the prow, searching in the darkness for somewhere secure to tie the rope.

Marko thought for a moment about being stranded on this hellish place, and then decided he didn't want to think about it anymore.

'Where's he gone?' he said, meaning Peter.

'He went that way,' Sorrel said, pointing away to the left slightly, to a dark shape that they knew was the outline of the ruins, and they followed. It was hard going, though they only had a short distance to cover. The ground sank beneath each footstep, a sticky, smelly, sucking mud that seemed to want to hold them back, but as much as Marko and Sorrel would have loved nothing more than to run in terror from their destination, they knew that their only path lay ahead.

The chant rose higher and higher with every step they pulled from the mud, and as it did so, another great shriek and wail was thrown into the night. Marko looked up to see a bank of sparks scurry into the night, and watched with fascination as the clouds of swirling and ducking sparks flew in crazy patterns. He thought they seemed to be forming a picture, some kind of definite shape, and

177

then, in a moment of complete madness, he thought he could see a face in the sky, a giant face of orange and white fire, leering down at them all, grinning and laughing.

It was the face of an old woman.

Marko pulled his eyes away from the sky and looked to see if Sorrel had seen, but she had her eyes on the ground, intent on finding an easier way to the ruined buildings.

'Sorrel . . . ?' Marko called.

She stopped and turned, keeping her feet where they were. Marko glanced nervously at the sky again, at the tower of flame, then thought better of it.

'Nothing,' he said. 'Let's find Peter.'

She nodded.

A few more strides brought them into the lee of the buildings, and a voice hissed at them from the shadows.

'Here, you clumsy fools! Here!'

There was no mistaking Peter's thick accent, and with relief they picked their way over to where he stood in the shadow of a crumbling doorway. Dog had already arrived and seemed for the time to have transferred his allegiances to Peter, almost as if he knew his chances of survival might be greater there.

'Let's take a look at our friends, shall we?' Peter said, grinning in a most unnatural way. Marko and Sorrel exchanged a look, but followed obediently enough as Peter led the way into the ruins. He turned and set off up a rickety flights of wooden stairs that still clung to the interior wall of the old place. Peter could not have moved faster up the stairs if he had flown like a bird, but Sorrel, and

Marko behind her, picked their way gingerly, testing each dilapidated step as they went. And they were right to, for the fourth step from the top collapsed the moment Sorrel put her toe onto it, falling with a crash into the dark below. She reached for the next and finding it good, practically jumped for the top.

Marko hurried after her and seeing the missing step clearly before him had soon joined Peter too.

They were outside. The upper storey of the building had gone, leaving a low misshapen wall on three of the four sides, and a floor of dubious safety. Peter seemed unconcerned, and strode to the naked edge of the building. Marko and Sorrel again tiptoed after him, and then immediately both shrank back a little as they gazed down at last on the scene that had been waiting for them since they left Giudecca.

It was an orgy, a riot, a party, a festival and carnival all in one. In the centre of an open space between the ruins of what had once been the centre of Lazaretto the bonfire blazed. It was enormous. Its core was a great white and red heart of fire that stood higher than two men. From here the vast flames licked up like the tongues of mad dogs, sending out the billows of sparks that Marko had seen from a distance. The fuel for the fire was wood from the many old buildings; floors, and panels and beams and joists. Marko wondered how many nights they'd been out here, and realised that the devils were slowly burning the place into nothingness.

Around this centre, every conceivable activity was taking place, as well as a few that were inconceivable to Marko. The whole scene reeked

179

of evil, sadism and vile happenings. Figures leaped, dancing round the fire, as well as numerous other smaller fires. They seemed drunk, whether on wine or the intoxication of their badness, Marko could not guess. Elsewhere, other bodies lurched round the open tops of vast wine barrels, almost bathing in the stuff in their eagerness to drink. Other figures groped and grappled shamelessly. Marko counted at least three fistfights, and on the far side of the square from where they looked, a brawl between half a dozen men was reaching some kind of conclusion. Marko watched with appalled terror as one of the men, a huge brute, maybe seven feet tall, picked up a hunk of fallen stone and dropped it onto a figure lying prone beneath his feet.

The dancing continued. Many of the figures were half naked, women whirled and danced in the firelight, their skin gleaming with sweat despite the cold and damp of the winter lagoon. Another fight broke out between two men, one of the dancing women trying in vain to pull them apart. She gave up and went off to join a group round a barrel of wine, while the two fighters drunkenly took it in turns to exchange blows.

Many of the revellers, Marko now saw, were wearing carnival masks, some plain and simple white affairs, others were ornate and splendid, with gold trimmings that flashed in the firelight. And others wore the demonic face of the three who had attacked them at Bruno's house in Canareggio.

From all sides, the chanting continued, rising and falling as more voices joined then gave up the tune. It was a baying, formed of syllables of nonsense. Yet somehow the chant spoke of the baser, more depraved things in life.

*   *   *

Marko glanced at the sky, at the tower of sparks, half fearing to see that dreadful leering face again, but with relief he saw only fire, this time.

'What's that?' Sorrel asked. 'What are they saying?'

Marko was about to ask her what she meant but then heard it for himself. The chanting from the rabble had finally taken on a meaningful sound, a single word, broken into three stunted syllables.

'Vam–pi–ri! Vam–pi–ri!'

The chant reached a crescendo as more and more voices joined, all now in perfect unison.

'Vam–pi–ri!'

'My God!' cried Marko. 'Are they all vampires?'

'What do we do?' Sorrel whispered to Peter.

He seemed not to hear, but stood, his toes inches away from the drop to the ground, heedless of everything. He gazed out over the debauchery.

'Is it safe to stand there?' Sorrel asked. 'Anyone could see you.'

'No one will see us here,' Peter replied. 'We are standing in the darkness and their eyes are blinded by the fire. Besides which, their minds are on other things. We could walk right down there and they might not even see us.'

Sorrel noticed he said 'might not'.

'So what do we do? What are we waiting for? Simono must be here somewhere.'

'Indeed,' said Peter. 'But first, we must see. We must see if She is here. Because I might just take

181

on all of these people, but there is only one I want to kill.'

Marko glanced sideways, and stared at Sorrel. His eyes were wide, and he dared not even voice Her name, but instead, he mouthed three words to Sorrel. She stared back at him, reading his lips.

'The Shadow Queen!'

9

'There!' Peter pointed, and following his stiff rod of an arm, Marko half expected to see the Shadow Queen herself, but far across the square, a group of figures had emerged from a building. They were distinct immediately, merely from their gait. These figures were not swaying drunk or lurching with hungry desires, but sober. It was apparent that they were about some business. There were six of them, but two were instantly recognisable; the first was the mass of flesh they had met the day before, in whose house they had been locked up, Nicolo Bruno. He made his way slowly, waddling into the square, looking about him as he went.

With him was an older man, thin, with a shock of white hair above his pale face.

'Father!' cried Sorrel. 'Oh!'

'Still,' Peter called, harshly. 'You can see for yourself that your father is well enough. He is alive.'

'I know,' Sorrel said, 'but . . .'

'But?' Peter said. 'Do not worry. I want him alive, as you do. Because he will lead me to *her*. Do you understand?'

Neither Sorrel nor Marko were sure they understood anything.

'What are they doing with him?'

'I'm not certain,' Peter said. 'They have something with them. Look! Do you see the man beside Bruno. He is carrying a box.'

'Yes,' Marko. 'It's the same one, I think. The one we found on San Michele.'

'And what is in it?' Peter asked.

'We don't know. It's something that Sorrel's father made for Bruno, but we didn't have a key. We didn't open it.'

'Why didn't you break it open?'

'I don't know,' said Marko, 'but I suppose, we thought we might be able to use it to find out something about our fathers from Bruno. If we had broken it . . .'

'Perhaps, but you should know better than to walk up to a stranger and expect good things to come your way.'

Marko thought about asking Peter if he counted himself as a stranger, but decided not to.

'Look,' he said. 'Something's happening.'

Marko was right. As the small group, with Bruno in its midst, made its way into the square, people fell still and silent. They seemed to be heading towards the great bonfire, and as they went the chanting and dancing, the drinking and the shouting were all gone.

Everything was suddenly quiet; the only noise came from the terrible crackling and roaring of the fire.

Bruno stood, impassive, as a crowd formed around him in a rough semi-circle. Marko began to count the figures now that they were still. He had

183

counted three hands worth before he lost his place, but knew that it would have run into the hundreds. From every dark door and alley, more robed figures stole into the night, every one as silent as the last.

It was an eerie sight.

And then Bruno spoke.

From their bird's nest viewpoint, at such a distance, and with the noise of the fire to obliterate the sound, the watchers on the roof heard nothing of what Bruno said.

He lifted his short fat arms up, to the sky, as if waiting for something. Then he pointed at Simono.

Simono himself stood, seemingly unaware of everything occurring around him. He made no move to fight or to run, and none of his guards seemed concerned that he would do any such thing.

Now Bruno pointed at the man with the box, and he stepped forward, holding the box high above his head.

There was a low murmur from the crowd, the first sound they'd made since Bruno had walked among them.

Bruno waved his hands, the crowd erupted, and a short but loud roar of pleasure burst out. Then, with great showmanship, Bruno rummaged inside his voluminous robes and pulled out a small object, holding it up for all to see.

'It's a key,' Sorrel whispered.

'They're going to open the box.'

They did open the box, but there was another shock for Marko and Sorrel first.

One of the figures who had followed Bruno into the firelight, swathed and hooded in a sumptuous velvet cloak of dark green, stepped forward. They'd paid this mysterious form no heed, but now, as all eyes turned to the figure, and as Bruno bowed low before it, the figure swept the hood of the cloak back, and Marko and Sorrel were horrified to see Venetia's beautiful blonde hair and face emerge.

10

It took a moment to believe what they were seeing, but there could be no doubt, even at this distance.

'My God!' Sorrel whispered. 'She's caught up in all this too?'

Venetia flicked the clasp at her neck, and the cloak fell to the earth, revealing her in all her glory. She was dressed in a shimmering green gown that swept the ground. Her hair was held up in a high stack, exposing her long white neck, and her delicate ear lobes, from which hung sparkling rings of gold.

'Is she a prisoner too, like Father?'

Marko shook his head slowly.

What followed was a bizarre pantomime, some kind of dumb mime-show that was played out as if for the entertainment of Marko, Sorrel and Peter.

The crowd seemed uneasy, restless. Bruno stood impassive again, resting his hands on his hips, his legs slightly apart. He stared at two men who carried a long narrow table into the arena, and set it down before him. Another man brought a smaller table of the same height, and set it by the head of the first one. Bruno placed the box on this smaller table, slid the key inside the lock, and with a flick of his wrist, unlocked it.

He whipped the lid back and even from their distant viewpoint, the watchers from the ruins could see a gleam and glitter as of jewels.

There was a murmur from the watching crowd, a growl of desire and expectation.

'Money?' Marko wondered aloud. 'Diamonds?'

'I'm not sure,' Sorrel said. 'Look.'

She nodded, and they watched as Bruno lifted something out of the box, and turn towards Venetia.

'The tiara!' Sorrel gasped. 'So he *did* finish it after all!'

'So why did she ask you about it? Outside your house?'

'Playing games with us. Evil games.'

They watched as Bruno took a step towards Venetia, and then, placed the tiara on her head, a vampire's coronation.

It was an awesome moment. Everyone was silent, the only sound the roaring and cracking and spitting from the bonfire. The tiara was spectacular. It shimmered like diamonds through the darkness, and was composed of five rows of glittering glass droplets, one above the other, which danced to the slightest movement Venetia made.

But Bruno wasn't finished. He beckoned a man forward from the crowd, and pointed at the table. The man sat on the table, then swung his legs up onto it and lay down. Bruno turned to Simono, then, who stood without moving, until Bruno took a short angry step towards him. Then Simono, as if sleepwalking, stepped over to Venetia, and

186

reached up to the tiara, and after a moment pulled two of the droplets loose from her beautiful crown.

Expecting Venetia to fly into a rage, Marko was stunned to see her smiling serenely as Simono turned to the man on the table. What happened next perplexed Marko even more. The man opened his mouth and Simono began to fiddle inside, pushing and poking the glass droplets into the man's mouth.

Now Venetia approached, slowly, languidly, and as Simono backed away, she moved in, bent over the man on the table, and kissed him on the neck.

A vampire's kiss. A kiss that hinted of death to come.

She stepped back, and Sorrel gasped as Venetia's face came into view once more. Her mouth dripped with blood. Luscious red blood, which she wiped away gracelessly with the back of a hand.

The man got to his feet, unhurt by the kiss. Ignoring the blood trickling down his neck, he stood up on the table and punched his fists in the air. He roared like a beast from the wild forest, and was answered by a deafening roar from the onlookers. Something twinkled in his mouth.

'What did your father do to him?' Marko asked.

'I have no idea,' Sorrel said, then she grabbed his arm. 'Look! They're doing it again.'

She was right. Another volunteer had stepped forward and was lying down on the table. Again, Simono, in his dreamy way, began to select another pair of droplets from the tiara. He turned to the man, who had already opened his mouth in expectation.

Venetia stood nearby, and even at this distance,

Marko and Sorrel could see her eyes wide with passion, her chest heaving with excitement. They watched Simono bend to his task.

'Is he helping them?' Sorrel asked. 'He can't be helping them.'

Peter turned to her.

'He has no choice,' he said. 'Don't be afraid. It is time to act.'

Nothing Peter could have said could have scared them more than those five words. What were they to do? What could they do against these dozens of lunatics and monsters?

'Don't be afraid,' Peter said again. 'I have work for you two to do. Take the dog with you. It is simple work. When you are done, come and meet me at the place where we tied our boat. I will have your father and we will leave.'

'It's that simple?' Marko asked derisively.

'If you do your part well,' Peter answered. 'Yes.'

'How will you get her father out of there?'

'Let me worry about that.'

'And what's to stop them just following us?' Sorrel asked.

'That's your part of the work. Go now, take the dog with you. They will be busy for a while down there, the box holds many of the things. That will give you plenty of time. Go back along the shore to the harbour, where we saw all their boats. You must sink them, every last one. Then come back to our boat, and I will meet you there.'

He clapped a hand on Marko's shoulder, spoke softly.

'Can you do it?'

Marko nodded, but Sorrel began to protest.

'But I want to come with you and help find

188

Father.'

'No,' said Peter. 'You don't want to come with me. Go and do your job well and that will save your father. You understand? You must sink every boat and ship. Yes? Now go!'

11

'I don't like it,' Sorrel said. They hurried as fast as the soggy shoreline would allow, making their way back to the harbour they'd passed on their way in. Night was drawing on, and they were exhausted already. Neither even dared to think about the task ahead, and Sorrel couldn't shift the feeling that she should have gone towards her father, not away from him.

'It's the only way,' Marko said. 'We can't help Peter. We can't fight, or do the things he does. He's like a ghost, a phantom, the way he moves silently and quickly.'

He paused, his eyes straining in the darkness. 'Look, I think there're boats ahead. Come on!'

They ran on, and found firmer land which rose to become a proper embankment from which the old planks of the jetties ran into the water.

'We can't do it,' Sorrel said breathlessly.

'We have to,' Marko said, but their task seemed impossible. Before them lay two dozen small boats, two rascone, large transport boats designed for the lagoon, and, worst of all, a small ship.

'We might be able to sink the boats, given all night,' Sorrel said, 'but we'll never be able to sink that brigantino.'

She pointed at the ship.

'Well, we have to, somehow,' Marko said. 'And we have to do it fast. It'll soon be dawn.'

Sorrel saw the glimmer of light on the Eastern horizon. It was only a pale gash in the curtain of black, but it was there.

'They won't stay past daylight. We have to work fast.'

So saying, Marko bent to the task. He tried the nearest boat, starting small. It was a burchiello, very much like Peter's in design. Marko tried to lift its nose, to tip the stern under, but couldn't move it more than a few inches. He gave up, and waded back to the shore, then returned, carrying a stone from a ruined building. It was as large as he could carry, and he smashed it down onto the bottom boards, trying to force a hole that would let water in and sink the craft. He didn't even make a scratch.

He tried a different boat, a small skiff, and this time began to push its side down towards the water. He managed to get the lip of the side to touch the water, and a little sloshed in, but then the boat's weight pulled it back upright.

Desperately, he turned to Sorrel.

'I might be able to do it this way, but it's going to take all night just to do one! Look at them all! And I can't even sink one!'

'Wait a minute. Wait,' Sorrel said. 'We have to think. There must be a way.'

But they couldn't see it.

Marko sat on the wooden planks of the jetty, defeated.

'If only my father were here,' he said. 'He'd know how to sink a boat.'

'But how?'

'He always says there is a way to do everything. But you just have to see it in a different way.'

'We need to get water into each boat, and we have probably less than an hour to do it.'

'No, we don't!' Marko said suddenly. 'We don't have to sink them all, we only have to make them useless.'

'But how?'

'The oars! The sails! We just have to get rid of them all.'

'Yes! That's it. That's it. But what about the big one?'

'I've got an idea for that too,' Marko cried. 'Come on! You start with the boats. Get all the oars and bring them to the brigantino. Throw them up on the deck.'

'Wait!' Sorrel said, 'Supposing they left someone aboard it?'

They looked at the small ship that lay at the centre of the flotilla of smaller craft. It was a low decked beast with higher poop and fore decks, and two-masted. There was clearly a cabin at the rear, and hold space to the fore. There were no lights aboard, but they crept up to it slowly.

'We don't have time for this,' Marko called, and taking the plunge, jumped aboard, and disappeared into the cabin at the rear.

Sorrel waited nervously, at any moment expecting to hear the sounds of a struggle, but a minute later, Marko emerged, grinning from ear to ear. In his hands he held aloft two weighty oil lanterns.

'We can do it,' he shouted to Sorrel. 'We can do it!'

191

Sorrel clapped her hands.

'Yes!' she called. 'Wonderful!'

'You get the oars, and the sails too, if you can. Throw them onto the deck here, and we'll have a bonfire of our own. I'll get started, then come and help you.'

Sorrel turned and waded to the nearest boat. Marko dodged back into the cabin, looking for flint and steel, but Dog stood on the jetty, watching the pinprick of light bobbing in the water, a little way off in the lagoon. He wasn't sure, but he watched it carefully. It seemed to be coming towards him.

12

Marko dragged a chair from the cabin on deck. It had a wooden back, but a small upholstered seat. He kicked the chair into pieces and laid them at the base of the foremast of the brigantino. In a moment more he'd ripped the covering from the seat of the chair and pulled out the wadding inside; a piece of hessian over a mass of horsehair; dry and perfect tinder. He smashed one of the oil lamps over the wreck of the chair, soaking the fabric and the wood alike.

He felt their luck was turning. Not only had he found the two lamps, but also a wonderful little tinder box, well made and ready to use. With his first strike of the steel he sent a shower of sparks onto the oil-soaked mess and within moments the whole thing was alight, dirty oil-fuelled flames licking up against the well-seasoned wood of the mast.

Sorrel appeared beside the ship and threw an oar onto the deck. Marko's plan was a good one; once the deck had caught, everything else she threw there would go up with it.

'Well done!' she called to him.

He laughed, knowing it could work. But he had to make sure, and with great care, he pulled out a burning chair leg from his fire, picked up his other lamp, and skipped back under the low doorway of the cabin. A second fire in here would finish the ship for good.

*　　*　　*

Outside, Sorrel found new strength as she sped from boat to boat. The oars were heavy though, and very long, so unwieldy once out of the water. She could carry a pair together if she was careful, but wished that Marko would come and help her soon. She made her way back to the brigantino and threw the oars on deck. Marko was still inside the cabin, and she turned and ran down the landing stage. She untied every boat she'd finished with, shoving them with her foot towards the lagoon, wrenching sails from masts, throwing oars into the water, dragging whatever she could towards the fire on the ship.

Then she turned, and screamed.

A man stood behind her, a lamp in his hand.

'Oh!' she said with relief. 'It's you. What are you . . . ?'

Without warning, he swung a fist and caught the side of her head. She reeled, but didn't black out. She sank to her knees and felt Francesco's arms scoop her up from the planks of the jetty, and carry her off.

Dog began to bark furiously, and snap at Francesco's heels. Francesco kicked out viciously, connecting with Dog's ribs, and he backed off, growling fiercely, but too scared to attack.

Francesco strode away with the dazed Sorrel in his arms, heading inland, straight towards the vampire camp.

Dog barked again now, louder and louder, running in circles, madly.

*   *   *

In the cabin, Marko was pleased with his work. He'd made a big pile of furniture and old cloth, and drenched it with the oil from the second lamp. He set it alight and was just backing out of the cabin when he saw Dog going crazy on the jetty.

Panicking, he looked frantically for Sorrel, and then saw the figure of a man, with a girl in his arms. They were a hundred paces inland perhaps, and then they disappeared round the corner of the first building.

'No!' Marko shouted, and without thinking, he and Dog were off in pursuit.

They thundered down the jetty, past the destruction wrought by Sorrel, and within moments rounded the corner of the ruins. A long dark street, lifeless for two hundred years, led away from them. Broken windows and shattered doors gave every house a haunted look. There was not a light to be seen anywhere. But at the far end, Marko saw the glow from the huge bonfire, and there, the silhouette of a man carrying Sorrel at speed, heading for the festivities of the vampire orgy.

He doubled his speed, and knew he was gaining on his quarry, but too late. As Marko put his hand on Francesco's shoulder, they emerged into the uproar of the square. Francesco spun round and recognising him, Marko hesitated.

'What are you doing?' he shouted, but Francesco dropped Sorrel to the floor and swung out at Marko. He parried the blow, but it knocked him off his feet.

The revelry in the square was reaching fever pitch. There was no sign now of Bruno, or Simono, or Venetia. With horror, Marko saw that their little altercation had been noticed. A few men, and a couple of drunken women stood nearby, but broke off from their wild cavorting.

They pointed, laughing as Sorrel and Marko got to their feet, backing away from Francesco, who suddenly pulled the neck of his shirt down, spinning round to show them his tattoo. With shock Marko understood. Francesco had been made one of them, had been called by the Shadow Queen, unable to resist her summons.

Francesco pointed at Marko and Sorrel, trying to get the vampires to understand that they did not belong, but his mute gestures and thrashings only reduced the others to more laughter. He turned back on the two and made a lunge for Sorrel, who dodged. Marko saw his chance and threw his fist, connecting with Francesco under his ear. He staggered, and they saw their chance to run, but now the others understood, and closed in on them. Hands grabbed at them from all sides, and though they fought back, it was in vain.

Suddenly the hands began to falter, and then they saw Dog, leaping and biting, snarling and snapping at those holding them. They tried to grab Dog, but he was too fast and slipped between them all like a twisting eel. They fell back, clutching their bites, still trying to kick at Dog, and missing. Dog had gone wild, and Marko and Sorrel looked about them, desperately weighing their chances.

They were still unnoticed by the mass of the people, but then they saw another flurry among the huge crowd. There was some kind of commotion in the midst of the crowd, and it was heading their way. There were screams, and shouts of terrible anger.

Two figures spilled from the throng. The first was Peter, swinging his sword in deadly arcs with just one hand. People pressed in on all sides, and yet kept their distance, watching the singing point of the sword. Peter's black cape swirled, and Marko had the strangest feeling looking at him. He was almost impossible to see, in the confusion and the darkness, with his black cape and the movement of his sword-arm, he seemed as hard to pin down as a ghost.

His left hand trailed behind pulling the second figure along. It was Simono. Peter held his right hand, and tugged him along like a mother dragging a small child.

'Run!' he shouted, breaking through the edge of the crowd. 'To the boat!'

Marko and Sorrel didn't need to be told twice, and with Dog's vicious attack aiding them, they wriggled from their assailants' grasp, and broke for the side of the square.

'That way!' called Peter, and they saw a gap

nearby, next to the ruined house they'd stood in earlier.

Now the shouts from behind grew more fierce, and they knew that the whole crowd was getting wind of what was happening.

Marko and Sorrel ran ahead, and behind them Peter came with Simono, fending off attackers with great sweeps and thrusts of his sword that threatened to take out five of them in a single swipe.

They rounded a corner and saw the boat, and seconds later Marko and Sorrel had it floating in the shallows.

Peter had lifted Simono in his arms and ran into the water, almost throwing him in.

'Start rowing!' he shouted, and turned to whisk his sword out again, as the first vampires splashed into the lagoon after them.

Marko and Sorrel took up their positions at the stern and prow of the boat rowing as hard as they could. Dog swam through the water and scrambled aboard. Simono lay as if in a trance in the bottom of the boat, while in the shallows, Peter sent several more vampires splashing into the lagoon.

'Help!' screamed Sorrel.

Peter and Marko turned at the same time to see one of the vampires had bypassed Peter and was grappling with Sorrel at the back of the boat.

It was the seven foot monster Marko had seen earlier, and he had Sorrel's arms pinned to her side. He pulled her head to one side, and exposed the long white softness of Sorrel's neck. He leaned in, his mouth opening, and Marko saw something gleaming where his teeth should have been.

Marko took two long leaps down the boat,

ducking under the covered section, and emerged with another stride at the stern.

The monster heard him coming, and turned, leering at him, showing a mouthful of teeth, with two long canines that sparkled like jewels. Without thinking, Marko swung his fist straight into the man's mouth and felt something break and shatter. The force of his momentum down the boat was enough to set the vampire reeling, but he rose quickly, and sent Marko tumbling with a single blow to the head. Suddenly Peter was there, and seizing the vampire by his arm, hurled him backwards towards the water. As he fell he lunged forward and sank his teeth uselessly into Peter's arm, where there was the sound of glass cracking; he fell back into the lagoon, as Peter put an end to him with the point of the sword.

He picked up the oar from beside Sorrel, and began to row.

With a few strokes, they were at sea, and though more pursuers tried to wade after them, the water was too deep. Some began to swim, but were soon left behind as Peter resumed the incredible speed he had displayed earlier that night.

By now, the whole bank behind them was filled with the raving mob, wailing and shouting in anger and hate. Then there was a sudden movement among them, and they began to run along the shore.

'They've remembered their boats,' Marko said.

'That is well enough, if you did your task well enough.'

Neither Marko nor Sorrel answered.

'Tell me,' Peter barked. 'Did you do what I told you?'

'Marko set the big one alight. We took care of the rest,' Sorrel said. 'We burned their oars, and sails.'

'All of them?'

There was a brief silence.

'Most of them.'

Peter grunted. He steered them out into the lagoon now, heading back for the city, but they could see the results of Marko and Sorrel's handiwork as they went. The brigantino had caught fire very well, and was a floating inferno, its crazy reflection burning in the water. The fire was so intense that it had set light to the landing stages alongside, and from there the fire had spread to many of the other boats.

'Maybe they're all burned,' said Sorrel. 'Maybe there won't be any to follow us.'

She picked herself up and ran to sit by her father. She put her arms around him and said nothing, but closed her eyes and listened to his breathing. His eyes were open, but whether he was drugged, or in a trance of some other kind, he seemed to take in nothing.

'Maybe,' said Marko, to himself, rubbing his fist. Small bits of whatever had been in the man's mouth sparkled in the bottom of the boat. He picked a sliver up.

It was glass.

He held it up to Peter.

'Look.'

Peter nodded, and then Marko did an extraordinary thing.

He laughed.

Sorrel stared at him, but then smiled with him.

'Glass teeth!'

'Glass!' laughed Sorrel.

'The fools!' Peter said, cursing.

'They've just been playing at being vampires. And Venetia playing too!'

'It was as I thought,' Peter said. 'They are not real vampires, but men making the pretence. And yet, despite this silly game, there is still her presence. They are under the control of the Shadow Queen.'

'Not Bruno? We saw Bruno down there, didn't we?'

'Bruno is her puppet. That is all.'

'But . . . what were they doing?'

Peter didn't answer.

Marko struggled to understand.

'So Sorrel's father made these glass fangs for them? Why?'

'What are they for? To be like the vampire they wish they were. Why did he do this for them? I don't know that yet. But we know that She is behind it.'

'Was . . . she there?' Marko asked. 'On the island?'

'No,' Peter said. 'I did not see her. But she is nearby, I think. Somewhere. Her smell is always in my nostrils these days. And you are wrong to laugh at her. I think perhaps there is a more deadly side to this game. Here, let me see that glass. There.'

He pointed to the bottom of the boat and Marko saw another piece resting in the bilge water. He picked it up and showed it to Peter, who inspected it closely, still without pausing his rowing.

'Look,' Peter said. 'Look carefully.'

Marko examined the broken glass. It had been

200

the form of a canine tooth. The tooth was unnaturally long, or had been, but the tip was broken where it had shattered against Peter's arm.

'Useless,' Marko said. 'It's like you said. They're just playing at being vampires.'

'Perhaps,' Peter said, 'they're playing. But maybe their games are deadly. Look closer at the tooth.'

Marko looked again and saw what Peter meant. The tip of the canine had broken, but inside he now saw a hollow channel, leading to a small reservoir inside the glass. A tiny drop of some thin green liquid still clung to the inside of this bulb.

'Be careful,' Peter said. 'It is poison.'

Marko gasped, and Sorrel turned from nursing her father, hearing the fear in his voice.

'How do you know?'

'Because some of it has entered the wound on my arm.'

Marko leaned forwards and saw a small puncture near Peter's wrist. The point of the glass tooth had entered and snapped off inside. Suddenly Marko remembered that he'd punched the vampire, shattering the teeth under his fist. He hurriedly searched the backs of his hands for cuts, but could see none. But the puncture in Peter's wrist was all too obvious.

'We must have a look at it,' Marko cried. 'It may have left something in you.'

'It did,' Peter said, 'but there is no time to waste. We cannot stop now. We must row to safety.'

He turned and looked back at the island. Daylight was edging its way across the lagoon, casting a hazy light on Lazaretto.

'I think I must ask you to help row, Marko,' he

said. 'They have found at least one boat that can sail.'

Marko turned and saw what Peter had seen. First one sail, then another nosed out from the burning harbour, and turned towards them.

'There is a good wind for them,' Peter said calmly, though it was news that terrified Marko. 'There is a good wind, and they can sail faster than I can row. You must help me.'

Marko did was he was told and skipped down the boat to the prow where he tried to match Peter stroke for stroke, but as he did so, he felt his arms turn to aching lead, and he knew that they would be caught.

13

They rowed for another five minutes, as the sun cast a pallid gleam across the dark water of the lagoon. Marko rowed until his arms burned, and Peter kept up his unstinting pace, but there was no doubt, their pursuers were gaining.

Without warning, Peter suddenly fouled a stroke with his oar. He recovered, but a few strokes later, did it again.

Sorrel watched him, fear growing in her.

'Peter,' she called. 'Are you all right?'

He didn't answer, but after a few more strokes, he stopped altogether. He bent double and took a few deep breaths. Marko turned from the prow, feeling their pace drop, and with alarm, saw, for the first time, the signs that Peter was mortal, after all.

'It's the poison, isn't it?' he cried, but Peter did not answer.

'Why don't we sail, too?' Sorrel called to him.

Peter slowly straightened himself, and shrugged.

'I do not know how.'

'But I do,' Sorrel said. 'Marko! Come and help me. If we can get this rigged up we'll outrun them yet.'

She sounded so sure, and yet, even as she began to fumble with the canvas of the sail cloth, she saw a single boat not far behind them.

Marko scrambled down the boat, stepping past Simono, who stared sightlessly into the brightening air. He mumbled something, which Marko didn't catch, too busy with Sorrel and the rigging.

'We have to get the sail out and hoist it with this.'

She put a rope in his hands.

'Wait until I've tied it, then pull when I tell you to.'

Sorrel tugged the sail from its berth along the deck of the burchiello and swung it across the boat. She hitched the gooseneck, and fiddled clumsily with the block, but at last she turned to Marko and almost screamed.

'Pull!'

The sail began to totter up the mast, immediately catching the morning breeze and filling. Marko felt the tug of the boat beneath him as the sail caught the wind, and they began to pick up speed once more.

Sorrel turned to Peter, who'd been watching her with a smile on his face.

'What is it?'

'You remind me of someone. You are clever.'

Sorrel was about to reply, but then saw with horror that the following boat was almost upon them.

'We were too slow!'

They could see the faces in the boat. Three men, all leering and calling to them, two unmasked, but one hidden behind that devil mask Marko had seen before. Dog began snapping and barking, sensing trouble.

'We can still make the island before they reach us,' Sorrel cried.

'Good,' Peter said. 'I prefer to fight on land.'

He didn't seem in any state to fight at all, but he was still their only hope of survival.

'There,' Sorrel cried, pulling the sail in tight, gathering more wind and turning slightly for the shore of Giudecca. Away to her right, not far, she could see her house, but she headed for the closest point of land, where a jetty pointed into the lagoon to greet them. The following boat was almost on them, and as Peter's burchiello crashed into the jetty, the other boat slammed into their stern.

Marko and Sorrel began to half carry Simono up onto the quayside, and he seemed able enough to follow, still muttering under his breath, while Dog leaped and ran, ran and leaped, trying to be useful and getting in everyone's way.

'What did he say?' Marko asked.

Sorrel held her father tighter.

'Are you all right, Father?' she whispered to him, but all he would do was mutter more of his nonsense.

'What did he say?'

Marko strained to hear what Simono was saying.

'Pentamerone!' Sorrel said. 'He said,

Pentamerone.'

Peter turned and backed down the boat, as the three Vampyri clambered aboard and crept towards him. They were unarmed, or so Marko thought, but then, as they dragged Simono to safety, he saw the man with the mask draw a huge curving dagger from behind his back. Suddenly all three came charging at Peter, who moved backwards down the boat, ducking under the awning, pushing his way past the sail and boom. Then he fell, and the man with the knife was on him, but Peter fell with the sword pointing up like a spike, which the man could not avoid. The other two came on more cautiously and Peter took his chance, struggling to his feet, unhurt. He waved at the two, and they edged backwards. Another wave of the sword and they edged back again, falling off the boat and into the water, where they began splashing noisily.

Peter sheathed the sword, and was about to turn to climb ashore when one of the men in the water managed to grab the side of the boat, and more by chance than design, tipped him into the water beside them.

'Come on!' Marko called to Sorrel, and they hurried to the water's edge to see Peter struggling with the two men.

They were a writhing mass in the water, and unable to do anything to help, Marko and Sorrel watched horrified as all three sank beneath the surface. Ripples and bubbles broke the water for a while and at any moment they expected to see the figures break again, but for a long time, there was nothing. The surface of the water grew still, and then there was Peter, pulling himself up to the light, gasping for air.

He struggled to the jetty where Marko and Sorrel helped him from the water.

'Those men . . .?' Sorrel began, but one look at the deadly gleam in Peter's eyes told her they wouldn't be coming after them.

Peter rolled onto his back, staring up at the pair of them, then sat up and looked around, still choking from the water.

'But where is your father?' he spluttered.

'Oh no!' Sorrel turned and saw Simono in the distance, heading away down the side of Giudecca.

'Where's he going?'

'He's heading home,' Sorrel said.

'It won't be safe there,' Peter said. 'We have to find somewhere to hide. Somewhere safe.'

But Sorrel was already running away down the embankment.

'Wait! Father! Come back!' she called as she ran.

Marko helped Peter to his feet.

'Are you all right? The poison?'

'I will fight the poison,' Peter said, and began to hobble after Sorrel, giving Marko no choice but to follow.

As they caught up with Sorrel and Simono, they were a few paces short of the steps to the Ca' Bellini. Sorrel was pulling her father by the arm, trying to get him to stop, but the old man was in a crazy trance, and calling that single word.

'Pentamerone! Pentamerone!'

'Father,' Sorrel cried. 'Please. We have to leave the house. We have to find somewhere to hide. Please. The Shadow Queen will find us if we stay here, her people will find us and take you away

206

again. Please!'

She sobbed and tugged and fought, but Simono would not be stopped. He broke free and ran straight into the house, crying out madly.

All three gave chase, following Simono upstairs, where he disappeared into Sorrel's room. There they found him, lying on the floor, his eyes staring wildly into space, his hand clasped around a book. Sorrel's copy of the Pentameron.

'Pentamarone,' he muttered to himself, almost peacefully now, as if he had found what he had been looking for.

'I don't understand,' Sorrel sobbed. 'What's wrong with him? Why does he keep saying that.'

'Simono,' Peter said, 'We have to leave. The Shadow Queen knows this place now. She will come back for you.'

At that name, Simono stirred slightly. He turned to the three, and for a second, his eyes almost focused to meet theirs. He proffered the book to Peter.

'Pentamarone!' he whispered.

Peter stepped forward and took it.

'Thank you,' he said.

Poking out of the side of the book was a slip of paper, tucked between the pages.

Something about it tickled at Marko's brain, like a face seen in unfamiliar circumstances that takes time to place. He had seen that piece of paper before, or maybe not that one, but another like it.

He reached inside his pocket and fumbled, pulling out the strange letter from his father, that he'd been clutching for weeks. The paper was thick, a dark cream colour, almost yellow, with small brown flecks in it.

Peter turned to face him, letting the book fall open at the page marked by the paper.

'There is a story here,' he said.

He read the title aloud, his eyes wide, his voice low.

'The Queen of the Shadows.'

He put the book down, and held the paper up, showing it to Marko and Sorrel, who was drying her eyes on the corner of her dress.

'My God! Is it true?'

Marko held up his letter, and they saw that they were like identical twins, their colour, their size, even the folds in them were the same. Peter read what his half of the letter said, and then handed it to Marko.

'Here,' he said. 'You had better read this. And then tell me, who is Venetia?'

Marko almost grabbed the letter from Peter's hands, and Sorrel leaned over his shoulder, and with quickly beating hearts, they realised they were looking at the first half of Alessandro's letter. Somehow the two pages of the letter had never been posted, had been separated, and while Sorrel had found the second half, they realised that in his madness Simono had hidden the first in Sorrel's storybook.

Now they held the missing beginning in their hands, and with it, the answer to their nightmare.

THE LETTER

My Dear Lady,

I write to you with a heavy heart, because what I have discovered pains me to my very soul. It has been, I am unafraid to say, a delight and a pleasure to have made your acquaintance over the last months since my arrival here to tend the health of my good friend Simono Bellini. Your obvious concern for his well-being touched me greatly from the start, and I must admit, your great charms have been a comfort to my weary limbs and sad eyes. To gaze upon you is to know the true meaning of beauty, and I am ashamed to allow that those private walks we took around the island on the rare occasions when my patient and his daughter both slept lingered long in my memory.

You are the most beautiful young woman in the world.

Or so I thought! And now, with my heart hanging in my chest like a withered apple on a barren tree, I write to you, Venetia, in the full and true knowledge of who, or rather what, you are.

*   *   *

I know what you are doing to Simono, for I saw you. Yes! I saw you steal across the space between the houses like some awful bird of prey, and suckle the sleep from him. All my own dreams and desires are gone now.

You have killed them, and replaced them only with terror, and fear.

A Fairy Tale

From that time on, the girl's heart began to shrink and to shrivel. She left the little hut and walked deep into the woods, hidden from all.

The years passed, and the young woman began to grow old, but still she could not forget her child, and she moaned and wailed to herself as she stole through the forests. And there, she changed. She became old and terrible, and no one ever saw her again.

Still she could not forget, and one winter's day, as she herself approached death, she cried out into the forest once more.

'Oh Devil! I know it was you who took my husband and my child. Come back now! Here! I demand it, and I am not afraid of you! Come back now and I will give you anything you ask for, only give me back my child!'

Then, she fell in the snow, and her eyes closed.

She woke, as she felt a hand at her elbow, and there was the old man again, though not a day older than when she had last seen him.

'Very well, Devil,' she said. 'That was a good trick you played on me. Well, now you can wave your magic again. Give me back my son, and I will do anything you ask. Anything at all. Only give him back to me.'

The old man smiled, the same smile he'd smiled all those years before, and his mouth opened.

'If I am to give you your son,' he said, 'I must have

211

something in return. I must have a soul like his, as pure and noble as his.'

'Very well,' said the old woman. 'I will bring you a soul.'

'No!' said the old man. 'Not just one soul. The soul of your son is worth that of many wicked men, and there are nought but wicked men in the whole of this wide world. For your son, you will have to bring me many, many souls. Will you do it?'

The old woman stared into his eyes.

'I will. But tell me, how many souls do you need?'

'One hundred thousand. Not one less.'

The woman laughed, and as she did so, the snow shook from the treetops and the ground shook.

'Very well. Not one less.'

*   *   *

No one saw her again, but they say that she keeps her bargain to this day, moving in and out of the trees, like a ghost, like a spectre, like a shadow. The Queen of the Shadows.

And they also say, that where she moves, death follows close behind.

But, it's only a story, and an old one at that, an old, old story.

FIVE

1

Through the tiny streets and alleys of Venice they ran, a motley gang. Two old men, one powerful but wounded, the other tottering along, his eyes wide, his mind stretched beyond the point of reason. With them ran a young man and woman, and at their heels scampered a flea-bitten mongrel, wondering what all the excitement was about.

They had fled the house on Giudecca, knowing it was no longer safe, and rowed across the canal to the main part of the city. Abandoning Peter's boat in the chaos of the moorings, they headed inland, to the very heart of Venice.

Marko's mind was a whirl. Venetia! What was she? Was it possible she was the evil that Peter had come to destroy? Could she really be the Shadow Queen who Peter ranted about?

There were many questions still unanswered, even more than before, but there was no time to consider them.

They hurried on.

'Where are we going?' Marko asked Peter, but the old man did not reply at first. Simono trotted along obediently enough beside Sorrel, too worried to care, as long as they were going somewhere to hide.

'Where are we going?' Marko asked again, tugging at Peter's sleeve. He seemed to be showing few ill effects of the poison, but had become even more taciturn than usual. Marko glanced at Peter's arm. Was he slowing? Was he struggling? Marko wasn't sure. He grabbed Peter by the elbow, forcing him to stop.

'Please. What are we going to do? Are we going to hide somewhere?'

'Yes,' Peter said, 'but not somewhere quiet. We are going to ground in the very heart of the beast. We will go to the White Lion, and take a room, but first, we need a little local aid.'

Peter turned to go, but Marko pulled him back again.

'Wouldn't it be better if we got Simono to the White Lion first? He needs to rest.'

'There's no time. We need protection. And I . . .'

He stopped, and Marko took his chance.

'Then I will come with you, and Sorrel can take her father to the hotel. We can meet them there. Please. The old man is dying on his feet.'

It was true. Simono was as a ghost walking now, his skin pale, his eyes staring, the pupils reduced to tiny dots.

'If we push him any more, he'll die. You may not care about that, but I do.'

Peter turned and stared at Marko, and for a brief moment Marko thought the terrible old man was going to strike him, but the anger passed.

'Yes,' Peter said quietly. 'I care. Very well. Sorrel, take your father to the White Lion, and get a room. Use a false name. Call yourselves Tomasini. You may have to pay well for a room, they will probably claim they are full. Do you have money?'

Sorrel shook her head.

'Then take this,' Peter said, and fishing inside his cape pulled out a bag of coins.

'It's all I have, so don't lose it.'

With that, Peter stalked on, and Marko was left

stranded between him and Sorrel, who stood mystified with her father.

'Hurry!' Marko said. 'We'll find you there by the name of Tomasini.'

'But I want to stay together,' Sorrel said passionately, and nothing she could have said could have given Marko more hope.

'And I want to make sure Peter comes back. That he helps us find my father. Don't worry. Just go, and go quickly. We'll join you soon. And take Dog with you. He'll only get in the way.'

He hurried after the retreating back of the old man from the land beyond the forests.

'Dog,' Sorrel called, 'Come on. Dog! Come here.'

The small mutt dithered between Sorrel and the rapidly vanishing Marko, then looked to Sorrel again.

'Dog. Come here!'

With that, Dog turned and trotted over to Sorrel, who held her father by the hand, while he stared at a wall nearby as if it was the farthest reaches of space.

2

Morning had lifted itself over the city's head and it was a fine, if cold, day. A fine day for the Doge's procession and all the other festivities that would begin at noon, and sweep the whole of Venice up in an orgy of excess.

For now, the city held its breath, as behind every door and window people made their final preparations for the carnival.

'Where are we going?' Marko asked Peter as they hurried through crowded streets.

'There!' Peter declared.

They were in a merchants' quarter, and stalls and shops lined the narrow streets. A canal, no wider than a single boat, ran along the side of the alley in which they stood, and people pushed by on either side, while others pressed into the stalls, haggling over everything. Peter nodded his head, so slightly that it was almost imperceptible, but Marko saw what he was looking at.

A few feet away was a workshop selling masks for the carnival. They hung inside the windows and on displays by the doorway, a mask seller ostentatiously flourishing one mask and then another, offering them to a pretty lady to try on, smacking the paw of a small grubby boy who fondled the goods when he thought no one was looking. The shop was surrounded by customers, and Marko understood Peter's plan.

'With the masks we'll . . .'

Peter nodded.

'We'll be invisible, like everyone else.'

'But they're very expensive,' Marko whispered, suddenly remembering that Peter had given all his money to Sorrel.

'We won't need money,' Peter said, and immediately Marko was filled with all sorts of horrible thoughts at what Peter might be about to do, but the old man turned to him and smiled, as if reading his thoughts.

'All I need you to do is fall in that canal. Can you swim?'

'Not very well. I . . .' Marko began, but Peter

was in no mood for discussion.

'Good,' he said, and with that, he took a step towards Marko and without another word sent him flying backwards into the water. Marko went under for a second, and began splashing and clawing his way to the surface.

He broke free and spluttered. The water was freezing, and rank, and he'd swallowed too much of it.

'Help me!' he choked as he went under again, then giving a mighty kick, surfaced. 'Peter! Help me!'

A pair of hands grabbed one of his wrists, and he felt someone trying to pull him out.

'I saw him,' someone cried.

'Saw who?'

Marko called again.

'Help me!'

More hands grasped his wrists and arms, and now at last he began to claw his way up the side of the canal, the pavement a few feet from the water's surface. He landed spluttering and shivering on the stones, and rolled over to see a large crowd gathered around him. He rolled onto his front and choked out the last of the water from his lungs. Peering between the legs of the crowd of would be rescuers, he noticed a tall figure in a black cape striding away down the calle, back towards the Grand Canal.

'Are you all right, my boy?' said a kind old man, his face full of concern. 'That was quite a trick you pulled.'

More than you know, Marko thought.

'Yes, I'm fine. I'm fine.'

He scrambled to his feet.

'I'd best get home and dry out before I freeze.'

And with that the pushed his way through the crowd, making his apologies, offering thanks, and then he broke into a run after Peter, who had already disappeared round a turning in the street.

Sword or no sword, Marko thought, I'm going to kill him.

3

Sorrel and Simono sat in their room at the White Lion. A fire roared in the grate and Sorrel felt warmer than she had done for days.

The house had indeed been full, or so the landlord had claimed, but the sight of five whole ducats had made him change his mind. With great grace he had begged Sorrel and the strange man with her to wait ten minutes, and then after the sound of an argument had risen to the level of shouting and banging doors, he had returned and shown them into the best room on the second floor, overlooking the canal. The room had obviously been recently occupied, but whoever had been staying there had clearly lost the argument.

Dog turned circles on the carpet, trying to find the right spot to satisfy him, but every time he settled, he would suddenly leap to his feet again, and start circling once more.

'Dog! Stop it! You'll wear a hole in the floor.'

Dog took no notice. Sorrel sighed. She went and sat by her father, who perched on the edge of a big bed, staring into space.

He had not said a word since she had found

220

him, other than 'Pentamerone'. She held his hand. It was clammy, and feeling his forehead, she knew he was feverish. His pupils were no more than dots, and his breathing fast and shallow. She stared at his face, from a few inches away, and found it hard to see her father there. It was as if he was already dead, already taken from her, and she had forgotten his face, because somehow his face before her looked nothing like her father. It had been the same when her mother had died. A face becomes meaningless once the life behind it has gone.

She buried her own face in his shoulder, throwing her arms around him, and began to cry.

There was a stirring above her head, and she looked up to see her father looking at her with his gimlet eyes. For the first time in months, he seemed to be trying to focus on something, on her.

His mouth opened.

'My child,' he croaked, and with that, his eyes closed and he fell back on the bed.

4

It took Sorrel an awful, long time to realise that her father had not died, but that the most wonderful thing was happening. He was sleeping.

His breathing was so slow as to be almost nothing, but as Sorrel laid her ear against his chest, she could hear the gentle rattle of Simono's lungs. Then the tears came even more quickly, and she rested like that for many minutes, until she was sure she was not imagining it.

In sleep, her father's face began to take on some normality once more, and without those mad eyes to distract her, she could even hear his voice as if he was talking right there and then.

Sleep. The only cure for his disease, and he had found it at last, away from Venetia's influence.

There was a knock on the door, and without warning, two masked men burst into the room.

Sorrel shrieked.

Peter removed his mask and laughed.

'Peace!' he said. 'We were just hiding our faces.'

'And you nearly scared me to death!'

She boxed Marko's ears, who pushed her away as best he could. Suddenly she stopped, and grabbing his wrist pulled him to the bed.

'Look! He's sleeping. Sleeping! Isn't it wonderful?'

Peter joined them.

'This is very good,' he said. 'Very. The rest will do him much good, I think.'

'Oh!' Sorrel said. 'Peter. I bought this with some of your money as we came to the hotel. I thought . . . I thought it might help.'

She hurried to the table where she picked up a small green bottle.

'It's called teriaca,' she said to Peter, who took it from her, a puzzled look on his face.

'It's for the poison,' she explained.

'I thought you didn't think it was any use?' Marko said. 'That it was a charlatan's gimmick?'

Sorrel shrugged.

'It didn't help my father sleep, but maybe it can help counteract the poison in Peter's arm.'

Marko shrugged. He turned to Peter.

'It might be worth trying. But do you drink it, or

222

rub it on?'

'I don't think it will help me,' Peter said, and handed Marko the bottle. Ignoring him, Marko pulled the stopper and sniffed it, as he'd previously done in Sorrel's room.

Again, his nose wrinkled.

'It's got such a smell,' he said. His face creased into a frown, and he took another sniff. 'But there's something about it. I think I've smelled it before.'

'Yes, you did,' Sorrel said.

'No, not then. More recently than that. Wait!'

He dug into his pocket and Sorrel gasped as he pulled something out.

'Do you still have that?' she said, seeing the broken glass teeth in Marko's outstretched palm.

'It's interesting,' he said. 'Father would love something like this.'

He held it up to his nose and tried to smell it.

'It's no good. Thanks to Peter all I can smell on it is canal.'

But Marko wasn't finished, and while Sorrel watched him, and Peter sat down on a chair, muttering, Marko hurried to the window, holding the tooth to the light.

'There's a little left.'

He dried the tooth with the hem of his shirt, then placed it on the table. By the grate, he found a slip of paper spill used to light the fire, and took it to the table. Placing the glass tooth on the paper, he took off his shoe and holding it by the toe, gave the tooth a smart crack with the heel. There was a minute splintering sound, and he quickly lifted his shoe away and smelt the paper.

'Here!' he said, offering it to Sorrel.

223

'I can't smell anything,' she said. 'Much.'

Marko offered it to Peter, who waved him away with a lazy hand.

'It's teriaca. Only not quite the same.'

'How can you be so sure?' Sorrel asked.

'This is what I do for my father,' Marko said. 'I mix his potions. I know how to tell one from another by smell, and colour, and certain other things. I'm telling you, what was in that tooth, that bit Peter, is teriaca, or something like it. Maybe teriaca with something else added.'

Then finally Marko made the connection.

'That's why it's not the same!' he cried. 'This isn't teriaca. It's something very like it, and we smelled it on San Michele. In the priest's room. This is the smell that was in those bottles.'

Sorrel understood, saw the picture at once.

'So that's why the teeth went from my father's workshop to Father Fei. He must have known how to mix the poison, and seal it into the fangs.'

Peter sat in an armchair by the window, but listened intently. He too saw the connections spreading out across the city, and began to see the deadly purpose behind all the charades that the Shadow Queen had made.

'But what does it do? Sorrel asked.

'I don't know,' Marko said. He looked at Peter. 'How do you feel?'

Peter shook his head.

'I don't know. I didn't think it was poison. From that tooth.'

'But how do you feel?'

'I feel nothing. I feel . . . tired.'

There was a note in his voice which Marko found hard to recognise, but then he knew what it

224

was. It was surprise.

'I feel tired,' Peter said. 'And that is not something I have felt for a very long time. Not since . . . Not since I used to spend a whole day in the forest, and swing an axe to cut down a tree, and drag the logs home with Sultan, my horse, and get home after dusk, and sit by the fire while my father drank too much. That was tired. That is how I feel, like I am going to go to sleep. Maybe for ever.'

His head hung, and his shoulders slumped. He ran his hands through his hair and if Marko had not known Peter better, he would have thought he was weeping.

Sorrel stared first at Peter, then at Marko.

'And that stuff is in every set of teeth that was in that box?' she whispered. She turned to look at where Simono lay on the bed, softly snoring. 'Oh Father, what have you done?'

5

Sorrel stroked her sleeping father's hair. Marko gazed out of the window at the Grand Canal, watching the fine boats make their way down towards the lagoon. Everywhere people in masks and the finest clothes jostled, a constant stream heading towards San Marco, and the piazzetta, to watch the arrival of the Doge in the Bucintoro, the magnificent ship which would bring him to his palace and to his rightful place at the head of the city.

Peter stirred in the chair.

Suddenly he rose and kicked the chair, sending it tumbling across the floor with a clatter.

'What is wrong with me!' he cried. 'I must act. I am so close!'

Marko rushed to Peter.

'Be still,' he said. 'We don't want to attract attention to ourselves.'

Peter ignored him.

'I must act. But instead we are sitting round nursing our wounds. What is wrong with me?'

'Is it the poison?'

Peter shook himself.

'It does not matter. What is wrong with me? I must act!'

'You mean to kill Venetia?'

'It is something I had not expected,' he said, nodding. 'Wherever I have gone, I have been hunting the old woman. She seems frail and pathetic, but she commands great power. She is an awful being. And I have followed her, but always she has been an old woman. I thought her power was weakening, but it seems I have underestimated her. She has found a way to become young again.'

'Venetia is the Shadow Queen?' Marko said. 'That's not possible. She's a young woman.'

'A young and beautiful woman, yes?' Peter said. 'Who has ensnared everyone she has met with her great beauty. Yes? Did you feel it too?'

Marko tried to hold Peter's gaze, but failed, feeling Sorrel's eyes on him.

'Yes,' he said quietly, looking at the floor. 'Yes, I felt it too.'

'Indeed. As did your Simono. And Alessandro too.'

'No!' Marko cried. 'That's not true!'

'You read it for yourself, Marko,' Peter roared. 'You read, in your father's own writing, the delight he took in walking with her. And you had in your own possession, that half of the letter that speaks of her true nature. Your father discovered the truth. He wrote it in a letter, but somehow the two halves were separated and lost. Yes?'

'But how? Sorrel, where did you find that half of the letter? The half you sent to me?'

'In Alessandro's room. He must have written it, but never sent it to her. Then they went missing, and I found it on the floor of his room. My father must have taken the letter, dropped half of it, hidden the other half.'

'Why would he do that?'

'It must have been during one of his worst spells of madness. He didn't know what he was doing, but perhaps he did really: deep down his mind was trying to make me see the connection to the Shadow Queen. To that fairy tale. Maybe even to Venetia.'

'But Venetia only arrived in the city . . .'

'Around the time my father grew ill,' Sorrel said. 'My God! Is it true?'

'It is true. She is the Shadow Queen. She has found a way to make herself young and beautiful again. She has used your father, and in doing so has caused his terrible illness. Sorrel! Do you understand? She stole your father's sleep. And with every night she flew into your house and sucked the sleep from him, she grew a little younger, and a little stronger.'

'But my grandfather died of this! And others of my family!'

'Then she has been coming here for many years,

whenever she has needed to free herself of the passage of time. I never knew this. I never knew, but I see it now. It is like I am with the sword. It has extended my life way beyond that which should have been mine. And this foul witch has been doing the same thing with your father, and his father before him, and so on and so on. Now we must find Venetia, and I will destroy her, if I can.'

If, thought Marko. Peter was usually so sure of everything he did. Why was his belief deserting him now?

'She's easy enough to find,' Sorrel said. 'At noon the Grand Procession for the new Doge will start. He arrives at San Marco and is taken to the Ducal Palace, and from there, he will gaze upon the ladies parading before him. The one he judges most beautiful will have the honour of sitting beside him to watch the Flight of the Turk and for the rest of the afternoon. Venetia will be among those ladies. That's why she wanted the tiara from my father, to wear at the procession. To make sure she won.'

'Something tells me she will win anyway,' Marko said, thinking of those lovely eyes, that delicious skin. Yes, he'd been fooled like every other man who'd met her. Like Nicolo Bruno, like Simono, like his own father.

Peter snorted.

'And then, she'll be in striking range of the Doge, with all her foot soldiers waiting to bite anyone who comes close enough. Pushing this poison into everyone of them.'

He smashed his hand across the mess on the table, sending the fragments of glass teeth spinning to the wall opposite.

'And what then?' Sorrel asked.

Neither Marko nor Peter answered her, for neither of them had an answer to her question, but then another voice spoke into the silence, and Sorrel whirled round to see her father sitting up on the bed, his eyes half open, as after a long and drowsy sleep.

'And then,' he said, 'she will control the whole city.'

6

Sorrel almost flew into her father's arms. 'Gently, my daughter,' he said. 'I don't feel quite myself.'

Sorrel laughed.

'But you're talking,' she said. 'You're actually talking. You slept. You're awake. You're *you*!'

'I feel much better than I have felt for a long time,' he agreed. 'That's true. Oh Sorrel, it has been a terrible thing. I have been in prison; trapped in my body like a prisoner in a cell. All the time I have been aware of what I was doing, what I was being made to do, but unable to stop it. It's been . . .'

He broke off and took a few deep breaths to steady himself.

'And Venetia?' Sorrel whispered.

'It is true. Everything this gentleman says is true.'

He nodded at Peter, who came and bowed graciously in front of Simono.

'At first, I could only wonder.' Simono said. 'I had not been sleeping. My illness had already

229

begun, but I had no idea what was causing it. It was then that I wrote to Marko's father, begging him to come and help. Then one night, I found out what was happening to me. I looked up from my bed to see Venetia standing in the room. "How did you get here?" I asked her, but she did not answer. Then. Oh God! She climbed into bed with me, and she bit me! The last thing I remember was her teeth at my breast, and then I knew nothing more. But I did not sleep. I spent all night awake, and yet in the morning, I had forgotten what had happened. The following night was the same, and so it went on, again and again, but each night I could barely recall what had happened. I grew into myself and became mute, and then Alessandro arrived. By this point I was a prisoner stuck in the living cell of my body, silent and immobile. One night, I do remember, Venetia flew into the room, and was sitting on my chest, when your father came in, hearing some noise, I suppose. He cried out, and Venetia fled by the window, but as she went, he cried out. He had seen the reflection of Venetia in the dressing mirror, and I knew he had seen her true nature, not the young image she had been projecting, but her ancient and horrible reality.'

'But couldn't you get anyone to help?'

'I could do nothing. My voice had gone, my mind was in the control of Venetia, and all I could do was watch from the bars of my prison cell. I have had to watch, as oh God! As she has done all manner of unspeakable and bloody things.'

Marko watched in amazement at the change in Simono. He had only ever known him as a mute madman, now he could see the man who was

230

Sorrel's father, he saw why she loved him. He was a kind, intelligent old man, with a delightful smile, though his eyes were still bloodshot and the pupils shrunken. Nevertheless, he was a different being altogether, and suddenly Marko was overcome by a terrible pang of loneliness and longing for his own father.

'Please,' he said, coming forward and kneeling by Simono. 'Do you know where my father is?'

Simono looked down at Marko, his eyes, puzzled, but with a flicker about them that showed he understood something.

'You are Alessandro's boy,' he said, and it was all Marko could do to nod.

'Then my son, I have something difficult to tell you. I heard Bruno tell Venetia that your father is to be executed. What day is it? Is it the day?'

'The day of the Grand Procession.'

Simono hesitated.

'I fear we may be too late. Nicolo Bruno is one of the Three but also one of Venetia's servants. He has arranged things for her. To get rid of your father and any help he might have brought me. Alessandro has been accused of blasphemy and witchcraft and is to be hanged at noon, as the opening entertainment in the festivities.'

'My God!' Marko cried. 'It's almost noon.'

'Then hurry!' Simono said, grasping Marko's sleeve. 'Hurry. Save your father, for he is my good friend. Hurry!'

Marko looked at Sorrel, who kissed her father's forehead.

'Will you be all right, Father?'

'Yes! Now go! Hurry!'

Marko and Sorrel rose to their feet, and saw the

231

door flapping wide, as Peter had already bounded away down the corridor towards the stairs.

'Hurry!' Marko called to Sorrel, and Dog scampered out of the room just as the door closed, and they were away into the city's carnival streets.

7

It was not that it was far from the White Lion to the piazza and piazzetta of San Marco, but the streets were tiny and they were packed with merrymakers, all heading the same way.

Marko and Sorrel had quickly caught up with Peter, slowed by the crowd, but he began to push his way roughly past people. They in turn shoved and fought back, and it was hard going.

Suddenly Marko saw one of the devil masks on a face a few yards away, and he tugged at Peter's sleeve.

'The masks!' he said, and Peter nodded, pulling out three masks from under his cloak. He handed one to Sorrel and one to Marko. Peter had not chosen particularly well, having only had a moment in which everyone had been gazing at the boy splashing noisily in the canal.

Sorrel wore an exquisite green mask with many beautiful feathers, suitable for a young lady, and it looked well enough against her black dress, but Marko's mask was a bird-beaked doctor's mask, with a huge curved proboscis that kept knocking into people's shoulders and wigs, and Peter's was another lady's mask, of pink velvet and looked obviously out of place on the giant man swathed in

232

black.

Nevertheless they felt safer inside them, and Marko was relieved that they pushed past two men in devil masks with no reaction from either.

They tried to hurry, and Peter led, bodily heaving people out of the way, until their complaints and angry cries threatened to turn into a brawl that would have stopped their progress altogether.

'What do we do?' Marko cried, his breath coming hot from under the beak of his mask. 'It's almost midday!'

'Let's try this way,' Sorrel said, and pulled Marko into a small side street.

'Wait!' hc cried. 'Where's Peter?'

'Here,' Peter said, joining them. 'Now run.'

'Where's Dog?' Marko called, but he was nowhere in sight.

Sorrel's alley was by no means empty, but she had chosen well, and it was easier to move. They elbowed their way along, and moments later burst into the piazza of San Marco.

As they did, the great clock above their heads began to strike the hours of twelve.

'We're too late!' Marko wailed.

'No! Look! They're late! They won't start without the Doge.'

Away, across the smaller square of San Marco, by the water, they could see the incredible sight of the Bucintoro coming in to its mooring. It was an extraordinary sight, a ship the size of a small palace, entirely covered in gold leaf and red paint. Banks of oars projected from either side, gracefully propelling the Doge's ceremonial barge into harbour. Crowds of people watched, cheering

233

and swaying, as Marko, Sorrel and Peter tried to push their way closer, but here the throng was at its most dense, and it was almost impossible to move.

Sorrel pointed to the far side of the piazzetta where two pillars soared into the sky. On one was a statue of a winged figure holding a spear, on the other a winged lion, the symbol of the city. As if in a nightmare, Marko watched powerless as the Bucintoro docked near the pillars, and a loud cheer rose from the crowd. The new Doge appeared on deck, made his way ashore, and was ushered through the gates of the palace. There was a long pause, and then he emerged again on the balcony of the palace, to the loudest cheer of all.

He lifted a small white handkerchief, then let it drop, and behind them, at the pillars, a drum began to sound. Now, Marko saw the gallows for the first time, and the sight of them spurred him on.

'Come on!' he cried. Peter was making headway at last through the crowd as people tried to move to a new position to get a better view of the Doge. He was dressed in magnificent ceremonial robes of deep red, with a comical little cap squatting on his head, above a hooked nose and wrinkled face.

Then, Marko's heart leaped. There, his hands tied behind his back, his head bowed, unshaven and unkempt, stood his father. Beside him stood the gallows.

'This way!' Marko called to Peter. 'To the pillars!'

'No,' Peter cried, 'There's only one way to stop this. Follow me.'

There was nothing Marko could do to stop him,

and despite his urge to head for his father, Peter led them towards the gates of the palace.

'Look!' Sorrel called to Marko as they disappeared under the balcony. 'She's there! Venetia!'

*　　　*　　　*

There was no stopping Peter, who seemed to have recovered his strength once more. As he strode towards the guards on the gates of the palace, he unsheathed his sword. The guards lowered their spears, but they were mere ceremonial weapons; clumsy, ornate things with pennants dripping from them. Peter slashed the tips off them, and the guards ran back through the gates, screaming for help.

By the time any help came, Peter was halfway up an internal staircase that led to the first floor balcony, with Marko and Sorrel close behind. A few officials began shouting at them and made to step in their way, but then they saw Peter's sword flashing in front of him and ran for their lives.

They barged into one room and then another, finding them all deserted save for bewildered servants, until they stumbled into a room with a balcony, packed with officials, and other noblemen and women. There were the Council of Ten in their black robes, others in the same style but red, and there, framed by the light from the square stood the Doge himself, flanked by Nicolo Bruno, and Venetia.

Everyone turned at the commotion, and there were shouts from outside, and the sound of running footsteps. The doors on either side burst open and guards, real soldiers this time, poured into the room.

'There!' someone screamed. 'Get him!'

Three men ran towards Peter, but after a sudden singing sound had cut the air, all three lay on the floor clutching bloody wounds. The assembled crowd gasped, as Peter moved away from the bodies, towards the balcony. More men poured into the room, and within four strides Peter was by Venetia.

She was more beautiful than ever, and wore a fine dress of light green silk, low cut and with bare shoulders, clinging tightly to her figure, sweeping down to the floor. Her eyes danced, enchanting everyone, but Peter turned to address the room.

'Stop the execution!' he shouted.

Venetia stared at him, and then a smile spread across her face.

'That is a strange mask for a man,' she said.

Peter pulled the mask off and threw it to the floor.

'Do you know me better now?' he asked her, and lifted the tip of his sword to her throat.

She smiled again.

'I know you, don't I? How old you have become!'

Her voice stroked everyone in the room, like soft silk, reassuring, sensuous and loving. She glowed like amber in sunlight.

'And how young you are,' Peter said.

'And am I not beautiful?'

Peter said nothing, and Venetia screamed at him.

'Am I not beautiful?'

Her voice tore into the room and as it did so,

everyone there felt a grave chill enter their bones.

More guards arrived, but no one seemed to know what to do. Several finely dressed noblemen crowded around the Doge, trying to get him off the balcony and out of the room, but the Doge seemed to think he should stay. Bruno was the only one who moved, screaming to the nearest soldiers.

'Kill that man! Kill him!'

Another five men ran towards Peter, who turned, brandishing the sword with such fury that they stopped dead.

'Another step and I'll take her head,' Peter warned and flicked the sword back towards Venetia, who stood motionless, her bare shoulders back, her head erect. Her hair fell in golden tresses around her long white neck, and the thought of her blood being spilled was enough to still the commotion in the room.

Marko and Sorrel edged around the side of room, forgotten in the drama unfolding.

Then Venetia spoke again, clearly and calmly.

'So why don't you?'

Peter turned to look at her.

'So why don't you kill me? You have been hunting me for years. You have wanted nothing else but to kill me, so why not? What is stopping you?'

'Nothing is stopping me,' Peter said, but Marko saw that the tip of the sword had just fallen an inch or two from where it had been before.

'Nothing?' Venetia said, her voice rippling around him, like the water in a limpid pool.

No one in the room spoke a word, all were frozen with fascination at the extraordinary sight of the beautiful young woman and the murderous old swordsman.

'So?' she said, goading him.

Peter tried to lift the sword, but again it lowered steadily more and more.

'Why doesn't he strike?' Sorrel said. 'What's wrong with him?'

Suddenly it dawned on Marko what was happening.

'He can't,' he said. 'It's her poison, it's infecting him like it's infecting everyone else. All he sees is a beautiful woman, not the creature she really is.'

It was true. Peter's sword tip was now resting on the floor, and his strength seemed to have drained from him entirely. As Peter gazed at Venetia, she changed again before his eyes, and took on another form, seeming to Peter to be the lovely olive-skinned girl from the long distant days of his memory.

'My love?' he crooned, as if in a dream. 'Is it you? Sophia?'

Around him, the guards began to close in, and Bruno roared at them to take Peter by force. From outside the sound of the executioner's drum suddenly stopped.

'Quick,' Sorrel said. 'We have to do something.'

Marko looked desperately around the room, and then he saw a glimmer of hope.

'Help me, Sorrel!' he cried. 'Quickly!'

He turned to the wall behind him where a huge mirror hung above a fireplace. Immediately Sorrel saw his plan, and each of them grasped one side of the enormous looking glass and lifted it from its hanging.

'Move!' yelled Marko, and so startled by the sound of his voice, the crowd parted as Marko and

Sorrel pushed their way towards Peter and Venetia, shouting as they came.

'Look, Peter! Look!' Marko cried. 'Look in the mirror! Remember what she is! Remember!'

They saw Peter lift his head and turn to the mirror, where he had a perfect view of his own reflection, as well as that of the hideous old creature who stood behind him. A wizened, shrivelled hag, with coffin-white skin and eyes that bled evil.

Seeing her own true form, Venetia shrieked and howled.

'Remember, Peter! Look!' Marko called, and Peter nodded.

It took him a terrible act of will, as in slow motion he lifted the sword once more, and sighed a single word.

'Sophia.'

He swung the sword faster than life passes, but it was not fast enough, and Venetia leaned away from the blow, still hissing at her own ugliness. Peter tilted the blade as it flew, and jerked his sword-arm straight. He struck home, and something gave under the tip of the blade. Venetia was pierced, and screamed in agony, clutching her side where the sword had penetrated. She backed away, and then in a horribly quick motion like a scuttling beetle, she sped to the balcony.

It seemed as if she would jump, standing on the balcony's edge, but instead she stepped out into space, walking through thin air.

Peter hurried after her and Marko and Sorrel followed, as everyone else in the room pushed after them in alarm. In the piazzetta below, the crowd had seen the incredible sight and began shouting and calling to each other to witness this unbelievable thing.

They saw Venetia running across the thick rope suspended between the Doge's Palace and the tower of San Marco for the Flight of the Turk, and more sure-footed than a cat on a wide wall she went, skipping along.

It sent a shiver up Marko's spine just to see it.

Peter climbed onto the balcony, but turned to Marko as he went.

'She must not get away,' he said. 'Go and free your father. She can do no more evil here. You will need this.'

With that he thrust the sword into Marko's hands, and then he stepped out onto the rope to follow Venetia, who had by now already reached the bell tower.

'Peter! No!' Marko cried. 'Don't go!'

But Peter had already gone. His strength returning, his skills on the rope were as unnerving as Venetia's, and he ran, barely bothering to use his arms to balance.

As Venetia made the bell tower, she disappeared inside, then reappeared on the second much longer section of rope, a vast hawser that ran from the tower right out into the bay where it was made fast to the mast of an enormous sea-going galleon.

Peter gave chase, and as he ran, he noticed the blood on the rope. It was black, unlike any blood he had ever seen, but it was blood nonetheless, and for the first time in his long dance with the Shadow Queen, he really believed she could be killed.

As he swung around the bell tower's balcony and set off onto the second rope, he saw that she was over the open water of the lagoon, but he also saw that she was slowing, and long before she reached the galleon he was on her.

Marko strained to see exactly what happened, but, in truth, there was little to see. For a moment the two figures grappled briefly on the rope, and then they fell, tumbling into the water with a splash that could not be heard.

Everyone on the balcony, everyone in San Marco waited, and waited for the two figures who had fallen as one to reappear, but seconds ticked by and became minutes, and then they knew that they were not coming back.

* * *

Marko turned round, Sorrel beside him, and saw a room full of Venice's rulers inspecting him. The Doge stepped forward, and Bruno with him.

Marko stared at the sword in his hands, not knowing what to do with it, holding it clumsily and with great fear. And with great fear, he spoke to the assembled room.

He lifted the sword a little higher, and Sorrel saw with a failing heart that its tip was shaking.

'Stop the execution of Alessandro Foscari,' Marko said, in a small voice.

Bruno stepped forward, half a dozen guards flanking him, and then, wiping his hand across his forehead, he answered Marko.

'Yes,' he said, sounding confused. He shook his head as if waking from a long sleep. 'Yes, of course. Yes. We don't execute people in this city any more.'

Marko turned to Sorrel, and, letting the sword

241

clatter to the marble floor, he put his arms around her.

'Thank God,' he said. 'Thank God.'

'No, Marko,' whispered Sorrel into his ear. 'Thank you. You did it. You really did do it.'

Suddenly there was another commotion by the door, a lady shrieked, as Dog bounded through the room, skidding on the marble floor and sliding into Marko's legs.

Marko looked at the ceiling.

'Wonderful,' he said.

'Oh, Dog,' Sorrel laughed, 'Where were you when we needed you?'

8

Of the moment when Marko ran to his father through the throngs of people in San Marco, and threw his arms around him, of the moment when Bruno followed as close behind as his short legs would carry him, and told the guards to release him, of the moment when Alessandro looked down into his brave son's eyes and told him that he was proud of him, Marko remembered little.

*   *   *

Of the moment when he and his father stood at the quayside with Sorrel and Simono, all four united at last, of the moment when Sorrel stepped forward with tears in her eyes and told him that she loved him, that she would miss him, of the moment when they stepped aboard the caravel bound for Piran

242

and sailed away, Marko remembered everything.

*   *   *

He had smiled to see Sorrel and Simono together, as they stood on the quay. Simono had slept again for fourteen hours, and then another twelve the following night, and seemed well on the way to health. He had put a hand on Marko's shoulder.

'Thank you,' he said. 'I have no son, but I would willingly share you with your father.'

Alessandro laughed.

'You're welcome to him,' he said, putting an arm around his son. 'There's eight more like him at home!'

Marko smiled, but there was something troubling him.

'Signor Bellini,' he said. 'May I ask you something?'

'Anything.'

'I read your father's diary. The record of his illness. There is one part that has puzzled me. The last five words. Do you know . . . ?'

'Yes,' Simono said, ' "Sunshine. Glass. Aurora. Wine. Simono." Yes, I know them, and they puzzled me for many years too, but now I know what they mean, for when I was trapped in the prison of my illness, I came to see that nothing else matters in life but the things you love. Those were the things my father loved more than anything in the world, and he wrote them down to preserve them for ever.'

Marko nodded, and smiled out of respect for Simono, but could find no words to say. He wondered what would be on his own list of five words, and then he knew one of them, as Sorrel stepped forward and whispered in his ear, and when she'd told him that she loved him, she told him something else.

'You know why you succeeded?'

Marko shook his head.

'Because you are your father's son. He taught you well, and though I thought you couldn't do it; you proved me wrong. And I'm glad.'

She stepped back again, wiping a happy tear from her eye, and then it was time to sail away.

*   *   *

'My son,' Alessandro said to Marko as the city disappeared from the receding horizon. 'What dangers have you faced to find me?'

But all Marko could think of was Sorrel, the girl he'd met who was never happy, but who he'd left smiling as she and her father waved goodbye and shouted their promises to see each other again. All the horrors he'd seen had gone now, all but perhaps one, and it was wrapped in oilcloth in the pile of luggage on top of which Dog lay snoozing.

Marko's thoughts turned to Peter. He struggled to even begin to understand what he was. But he had been there when they needed him, and he had seen his promise to the Shadow Queen through to the bitter end. Marko made his way to the side of the ship and gazed at the water, then began to untie something from their bundle of belongings.

Dog stirred and opened one eye, but shut it again quickly, already feeling very uneasy about sea travel.

'In three days we'll be home,' Alessandro said,

coming up beside Marko, but Marko did not answer. He untied the oilcloth package, and took out the sword in its scabbard.

He pulled the blade a few inches clear and they gazed at the burnished metal. Was it evil, or was it good? Perhaps it had done much of both, Marko decided, but he knew what he had to do with it.

'It's beautiful, isn't it?' Alessandro said.

Marko nodded, then slid the sword back into its home, and wrapped it up tightly once more. Then, without ceremony, he turned and dropped it over the side, into the water.

'Yes, Father,' Marko said, 'but it is other things as well. And it doesn't belong with us.'

For a brief second the sword was visible beneath the water's surface, and then it was gone for ever, falling down, down and down to join the dark things lurking at the bottom of the deepest depths of the sea.

Death can come in many forms, but in Venice, death comes by water.